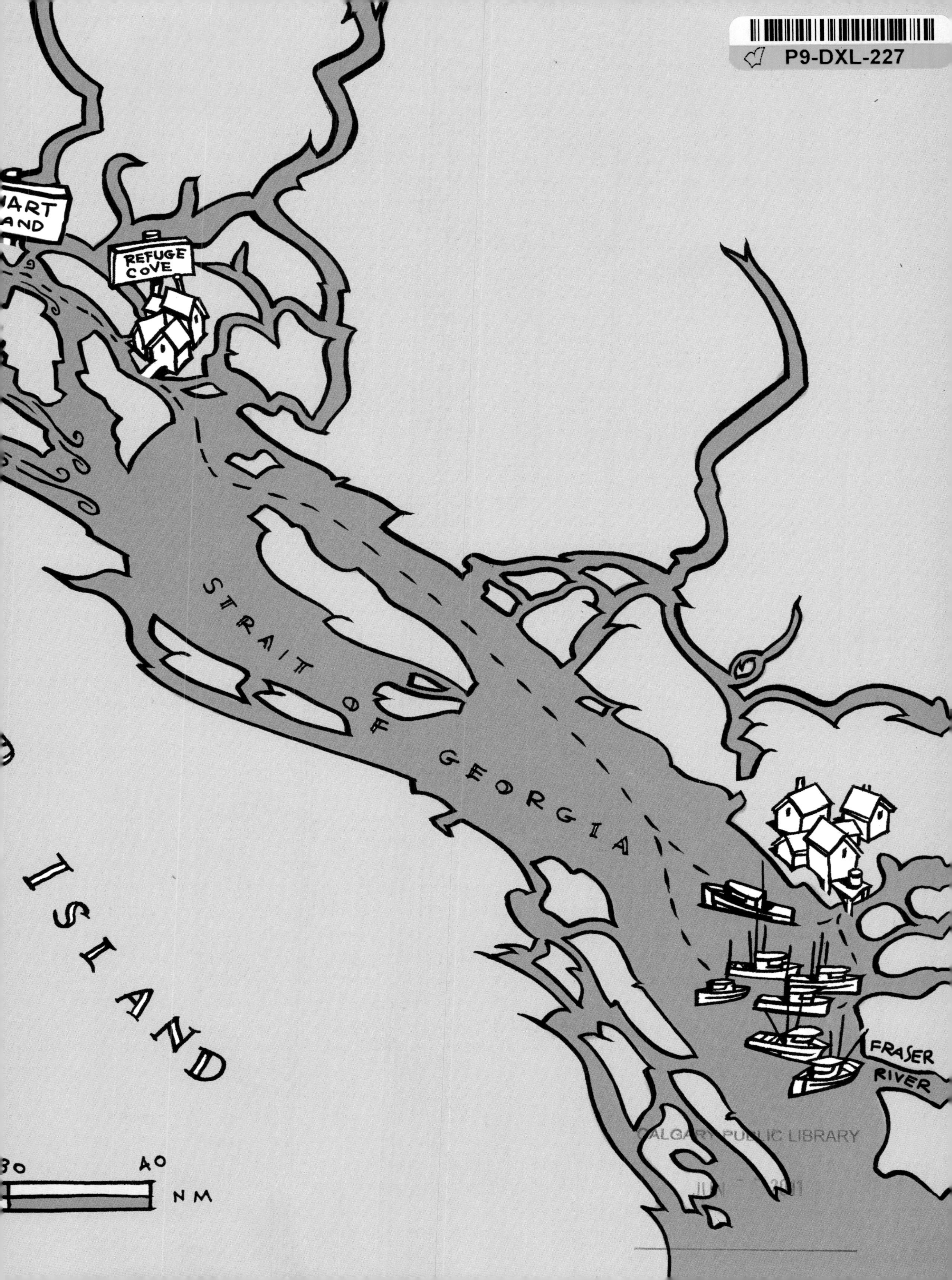
REFUGE COVE
STRAIT OF GEORGIA
ISLAND
FRASER RIVER
40
NM

Fishing with Gubby

by Gary Kent
illustrated by Kim La Fave

Harbour Publishing

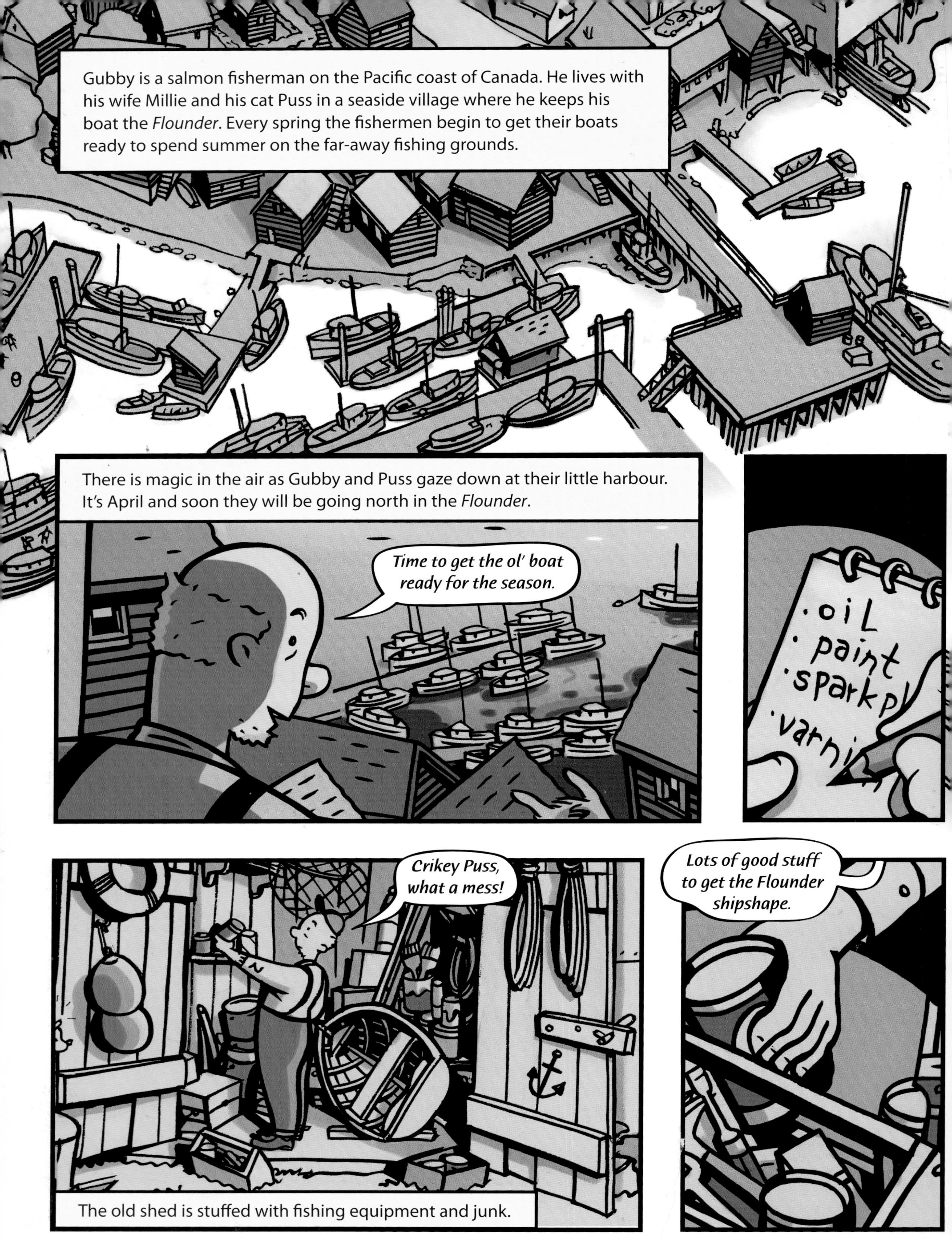

Gubby is a salmon fisherman on the Pacific coast of Canada. He lives with his wife Millie and his cat Puss in a seaside village where he keeps his boat the *Flounder*. Every spring the fishermen begin to get their boats ready to spend summer on the far-away fishing grounds.
There is magic in the air as Gubby and Puss gaze down at their little harbour. It's April and soon they will be going north in the *Flounder*.
Time to get the ol' boat ready for the season.
·oiL
·paint
·sparkpl
·varni
Crikey Puss, what a mess!
The old shed is stuffed with fishing equipment and junk.
Lots of good stuff to get the Flounder shipshape.

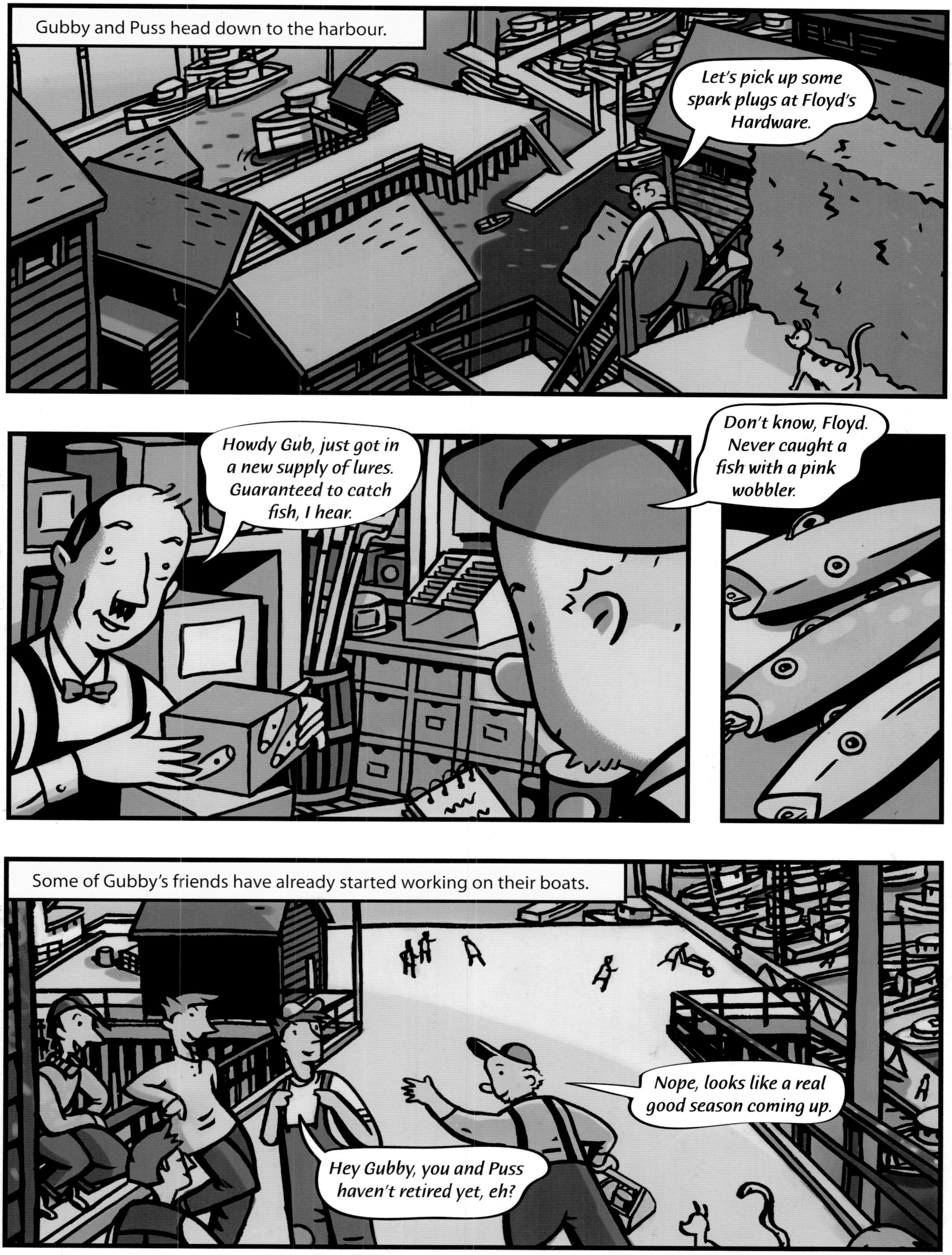
Gubby and Puss head down to the harbour.
Let's pick up some spark plugs at Floyd's Hardware.
Howdy Gub, just got in a new supply of lures. Guaranteed to catch fish, I hear.
Don't know, Floyd. Never caught a fish with a pink wobbler.
Some of Gubby's friends have already started working on their boats.
Hey Gubby, you and Puss haven't retired yet, eh?
Nope, looks like a real good season coming up.

The wharf in springtime is a beehive of activity. Fishing boats of every size and shape are being fixed and painted for the upcoming salmon season. Tugs and log salvage boats are coming and going. Floatplanes are dropping off and picking up people from all over the coast.

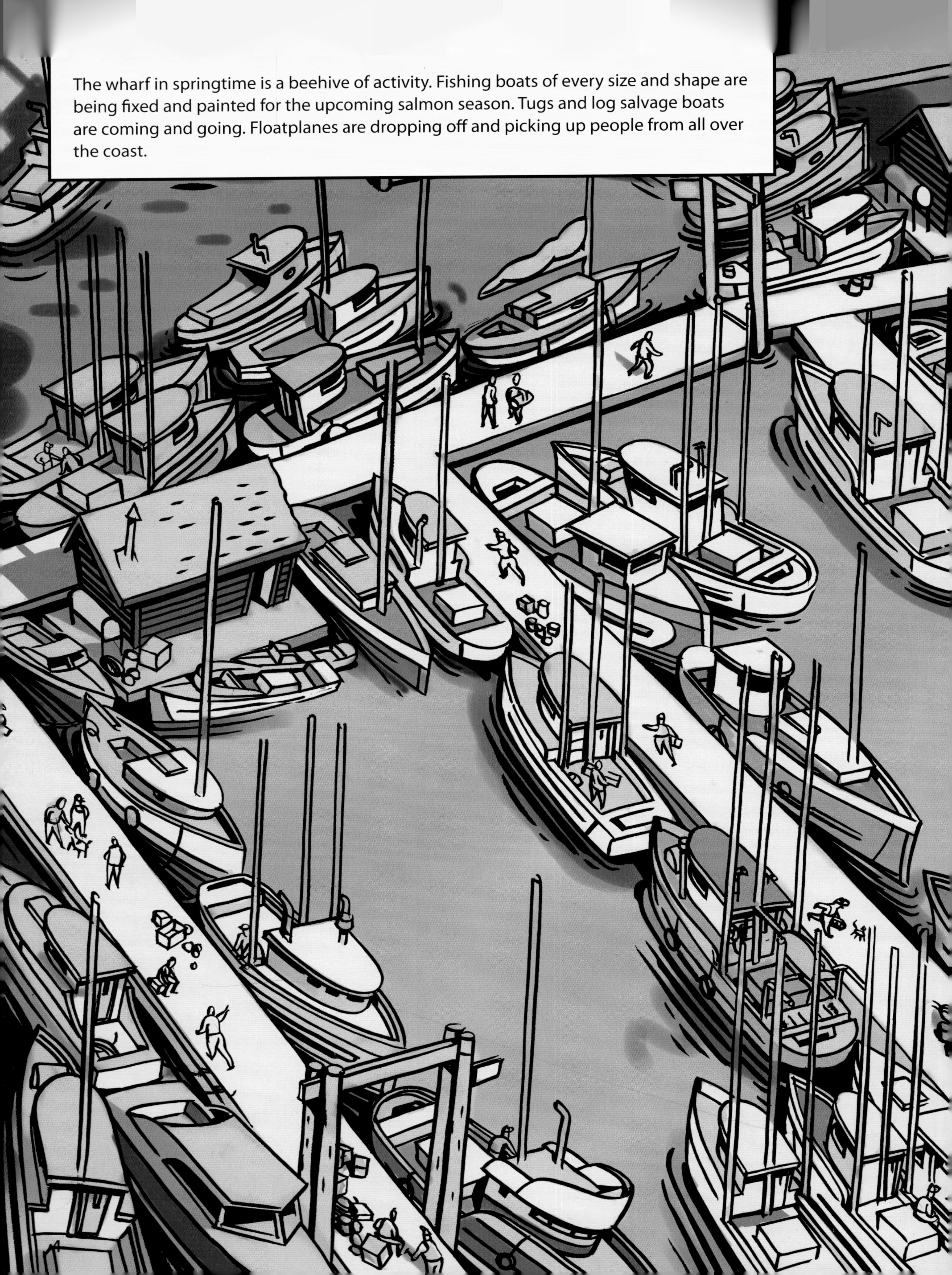

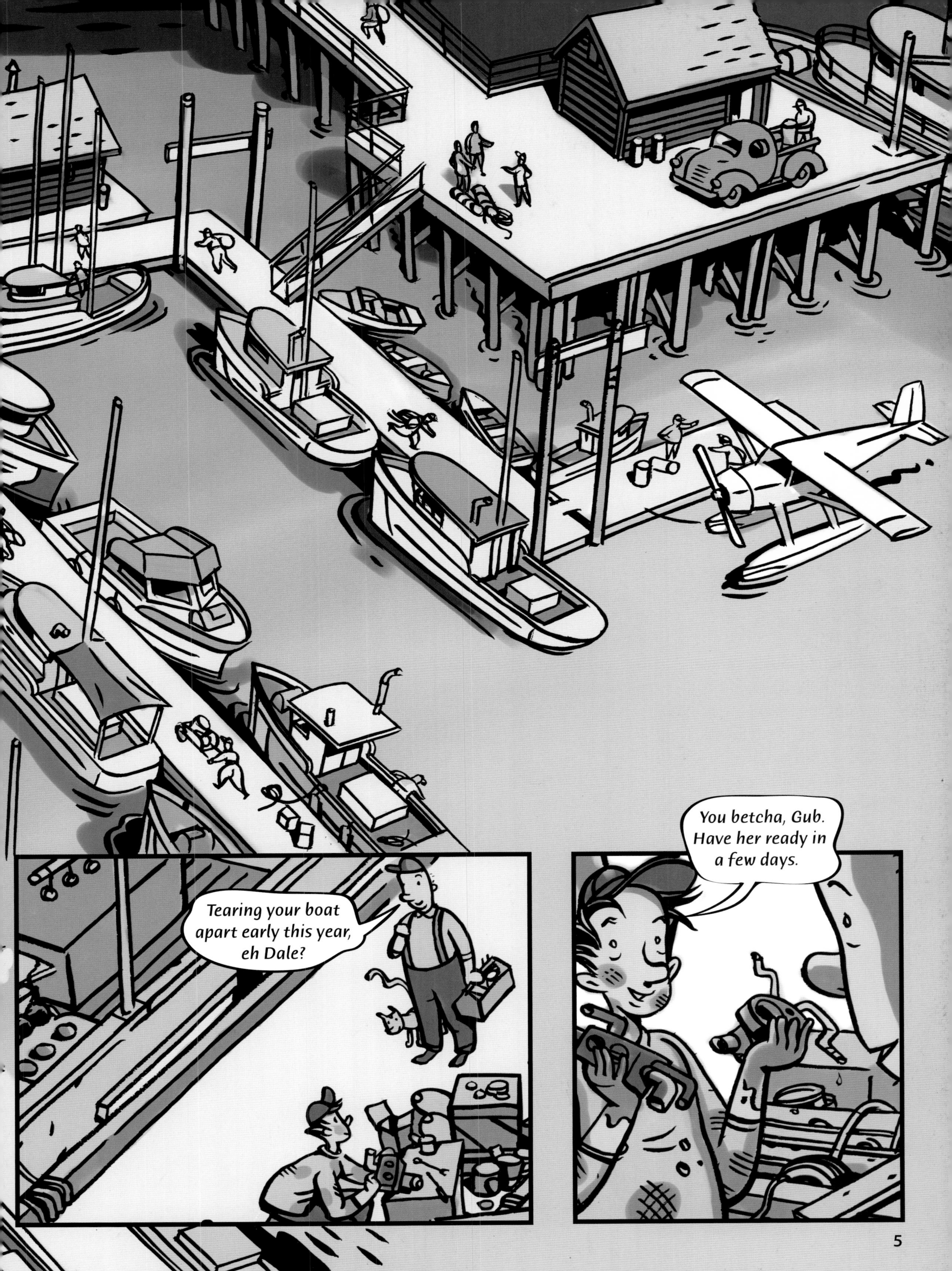
Tearing your boat apart early this year, eh Dale?
You betcha, Gub. Have her ready in a few days.

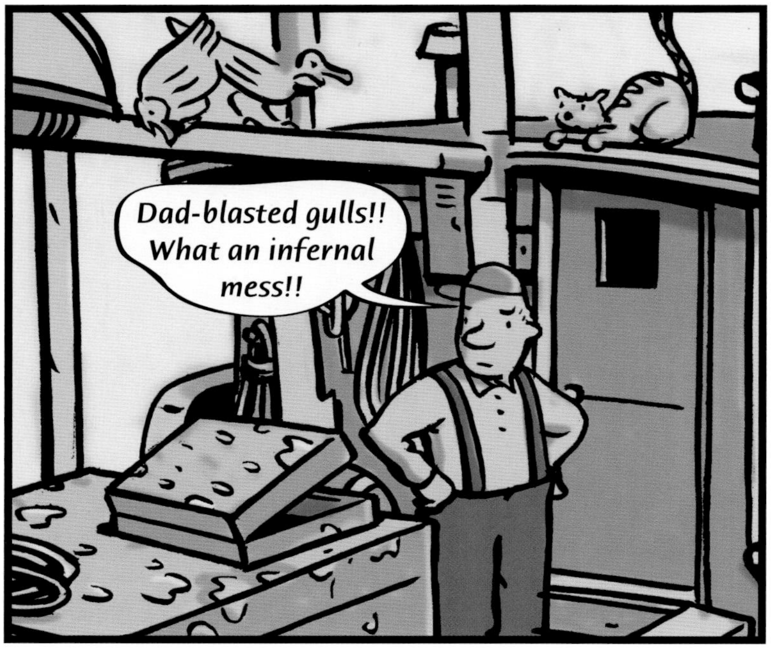
Dad-blasted gulls!! What an infernal mess!!

Flounder is not looking so good after sitting at the wharf all winter long. Rain, snow, saltwater and seagulls have made quite a mess of the little boat.

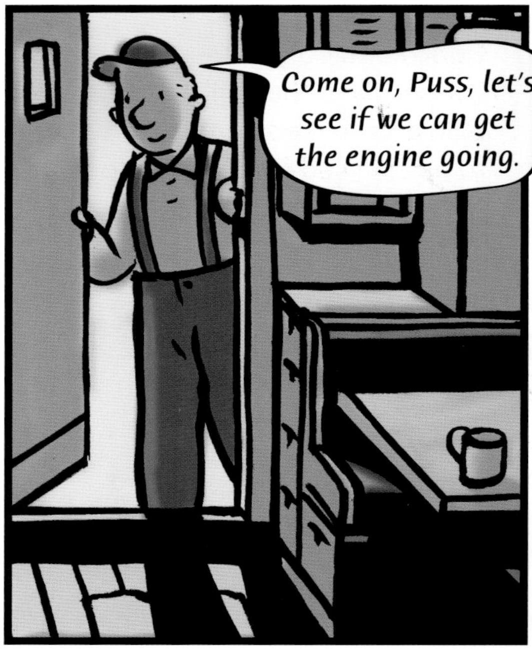
Come on, Puss, let's see if we can get the engine going.

Gubby needs to scrape the barnacles off the bottom of the boat and then paint it. To do this he takes the *Flounder* to the grid which is a flat place on the beach for working on boats.

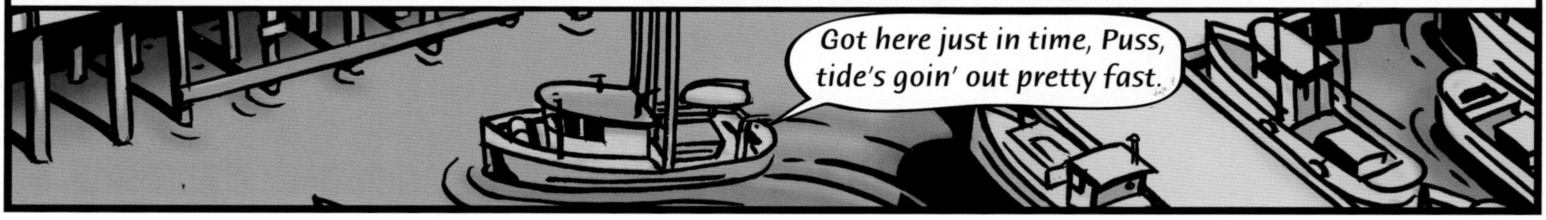
Got here just in time, Puss, tide's goin' out pretty fast.

Gubby places the *Flounder* over the grid and ties up to the wharf pilings just as the tide begins to fall.

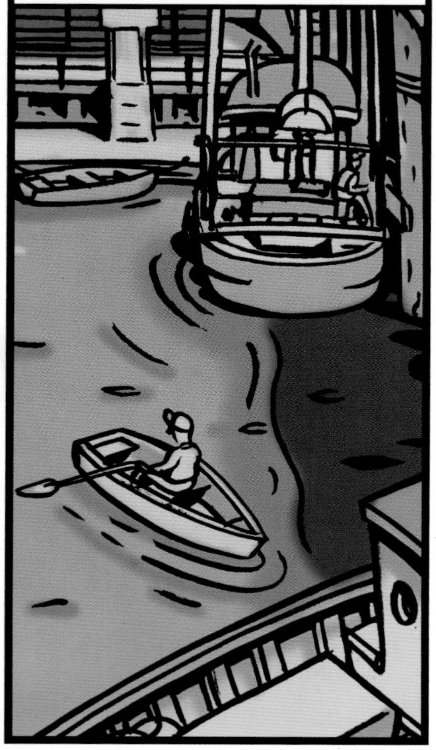

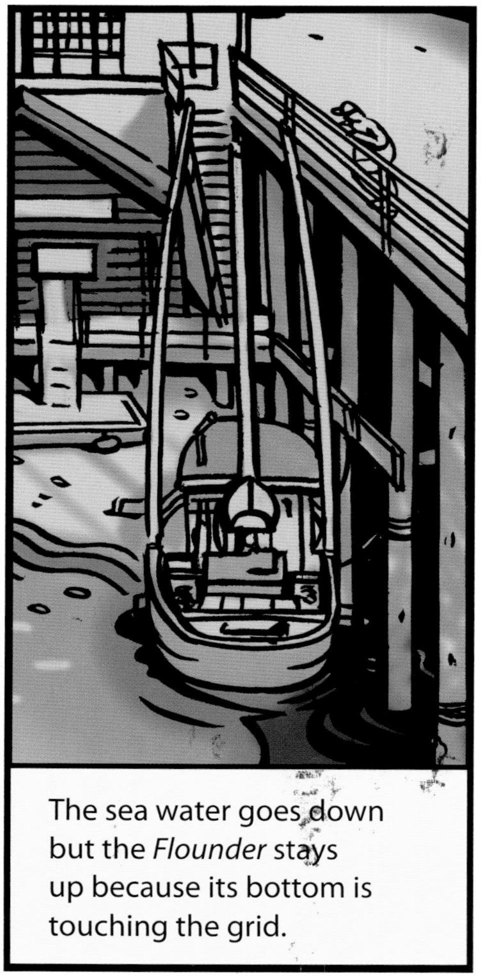

The sea water goes down but the *Flounder* stays up because its bottom is touching the grid.

The bottom of the boat is dripping with seaweed and barnacles.

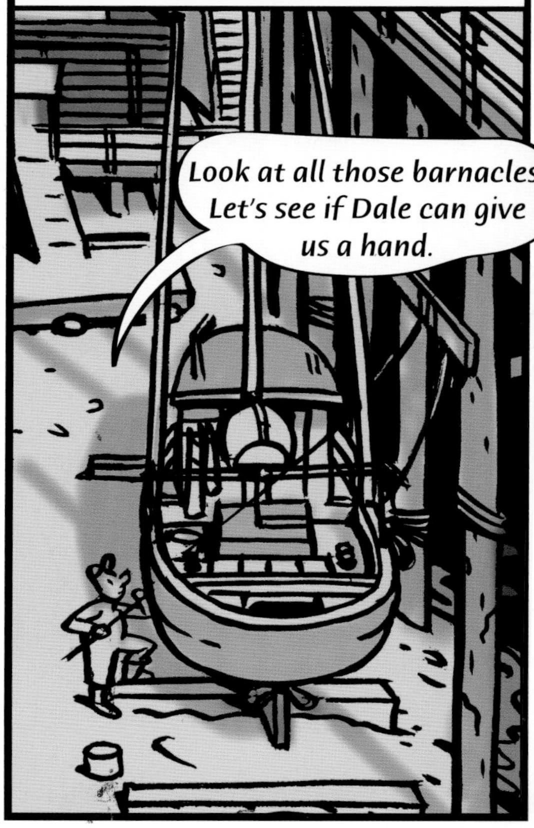
Look at all those barnacles. Let's see if Dale can give us a hand.

Gubby and Dale have to work really fast before the tide comes back in six hours later. They use a special copper paint that will keep the barnacles from growing back, at least for awhile. They also check the bottom planks to make sure that none have been damaged from banging into rocks. The propeller and rudder need to be checked for damage, too.

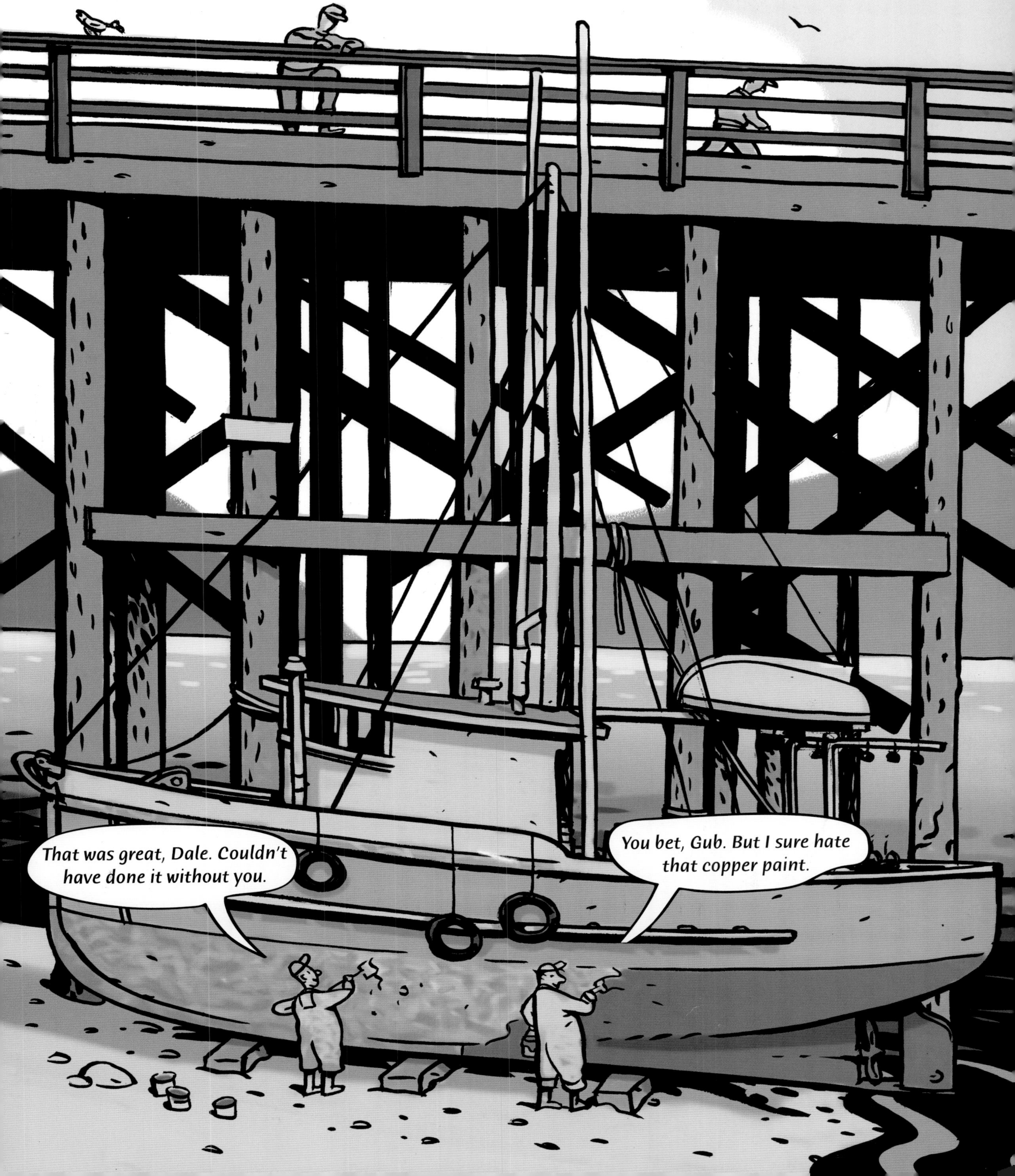
That was great, Dale. Couldn't have done it without you.
You bet, Gub. But I sure hate that copper paint.

Gubby feels good that the boat's bottom has been painted. He can now get busy on the rest of the boat.

The *Flounder* is a 36-foot (12-metre) West Coast salmon troller with a 6-cylinder gas engine that pushes the boat along at a good steady 7 knots, which is about as fast as a person can run. Trollers use lines and hooks to catch fish. Seiners and gillnetters, the other types of salmon-fishing boats, use nets. Fishing boats are work boats and not usually very comfortable to live in but Gubby is a carpenter in the winter and has made the boat very cozy for him and Puss.

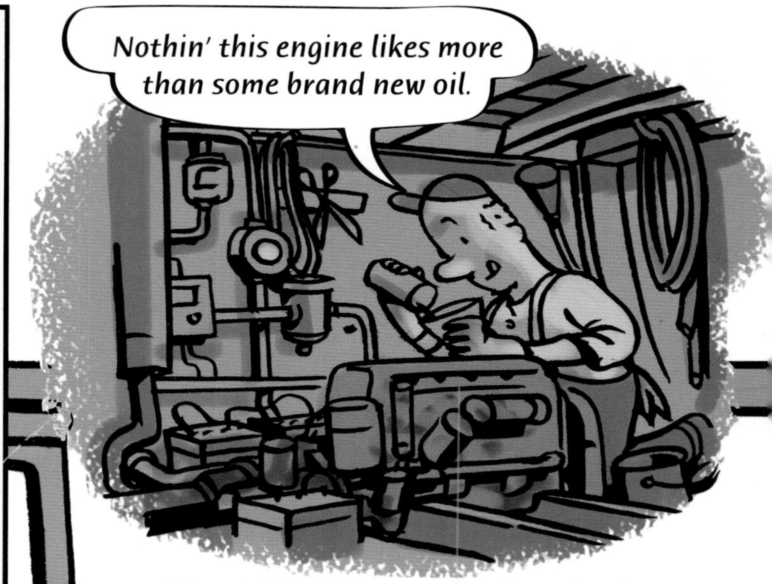
Nothin' this engine likes more than some brand new oil.

The old filter and engine oil need to be replaced.

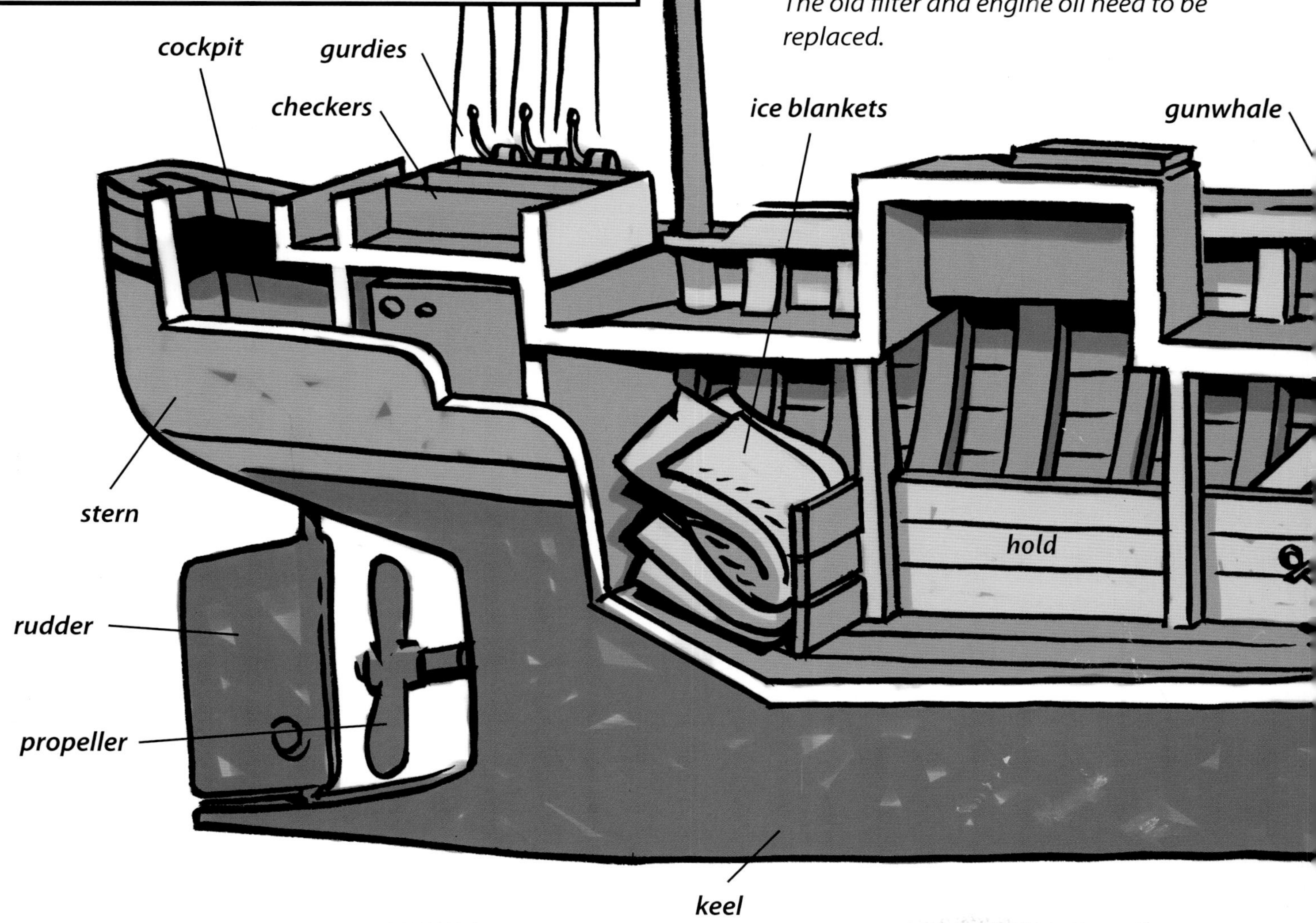
cockpit
gurdies
checkers
ice blankets
gunwhale
stern
hold
rudder
propeller
keel

The Flounder *has tall wooden poles that need to be lowered onto the wharf so that Gubby can inspect them for rot and cracks. At the end of the poles are springs and bells that make a noise when a fish is on the line.*

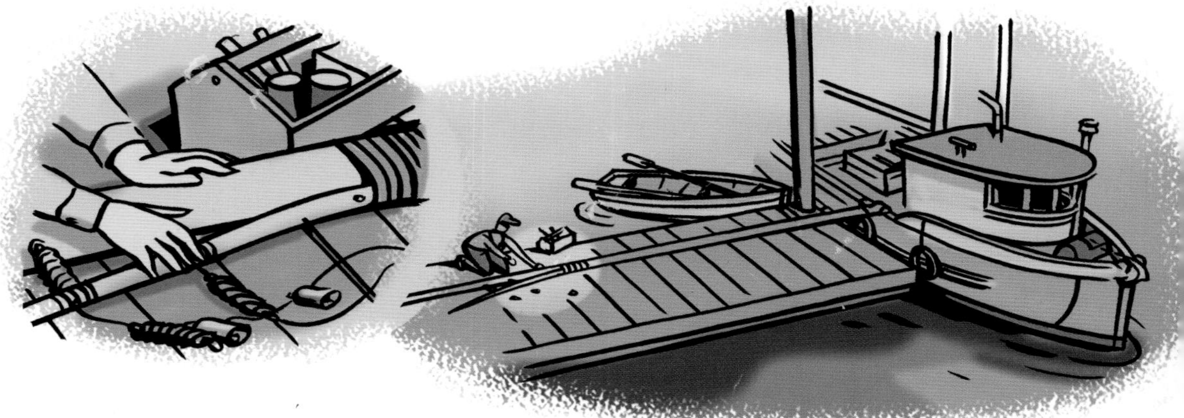

Then he checks his fishing gear. Everything must be kept in good working order. Hooks need to be sharp and lures—wobblers, plugs, flashers and hoochies—need to be clean and shiny.

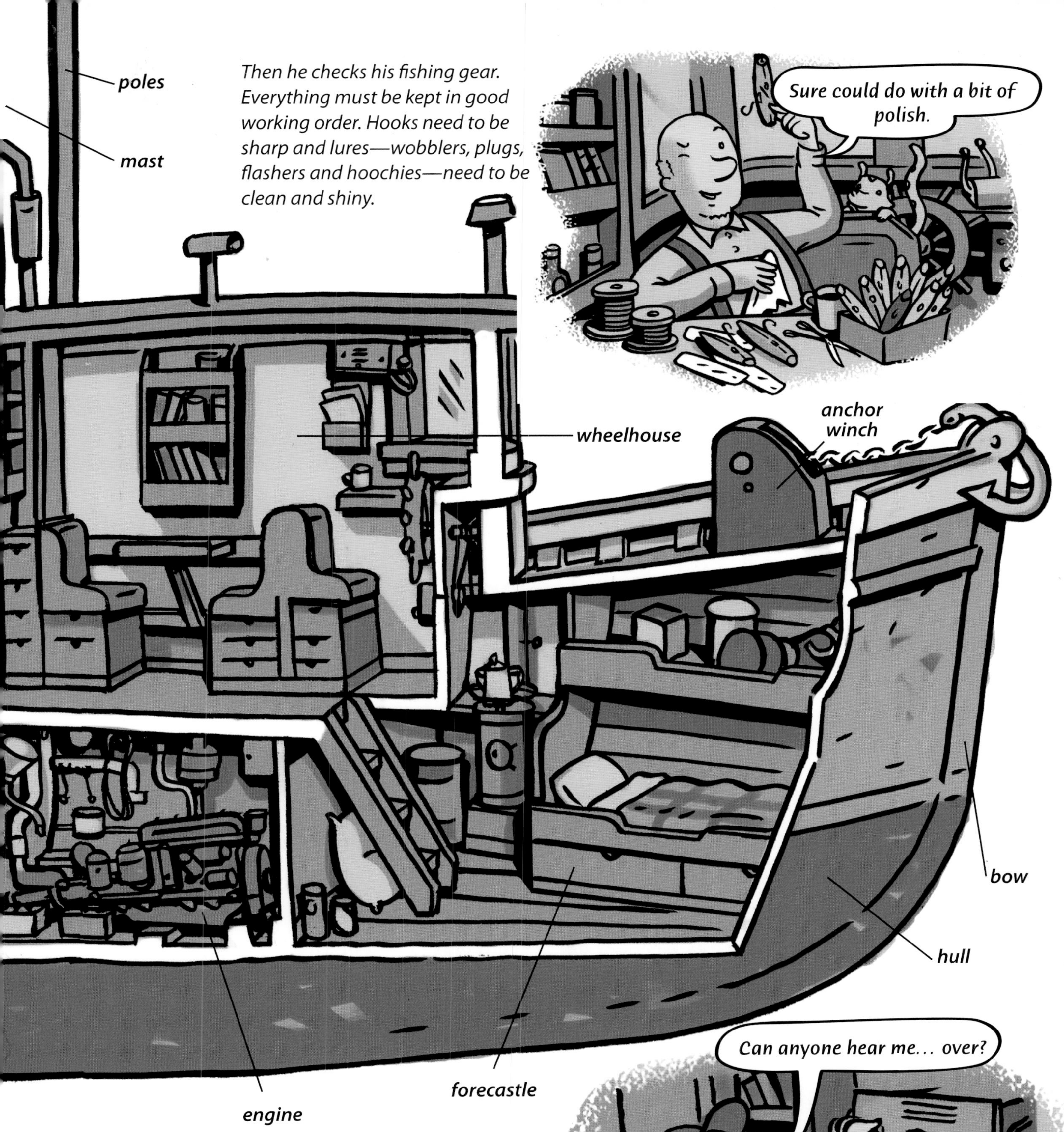

poles
mast
wheelhouse
anchor winch
bow
hull
forecastle
engine
Sure could do with a bit of polish.

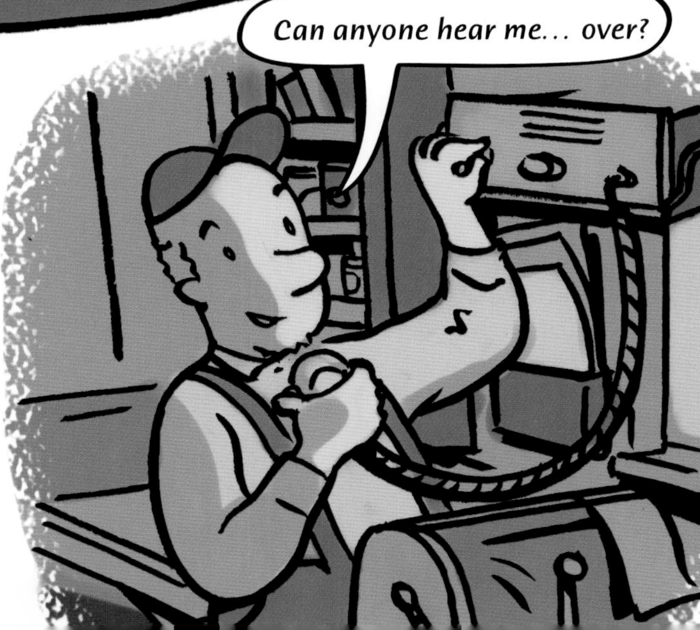

Can anyone hear me... over?

Gubby makes sure that his trusty old radio telephone still works. He likes to phone Millie and his fishing pals and if the *Flounder's* engine quits he will need it to call for help.

After weeks of hard work Gubby and his wife Millie look with pride at how wonderful the *Flounder* looks.

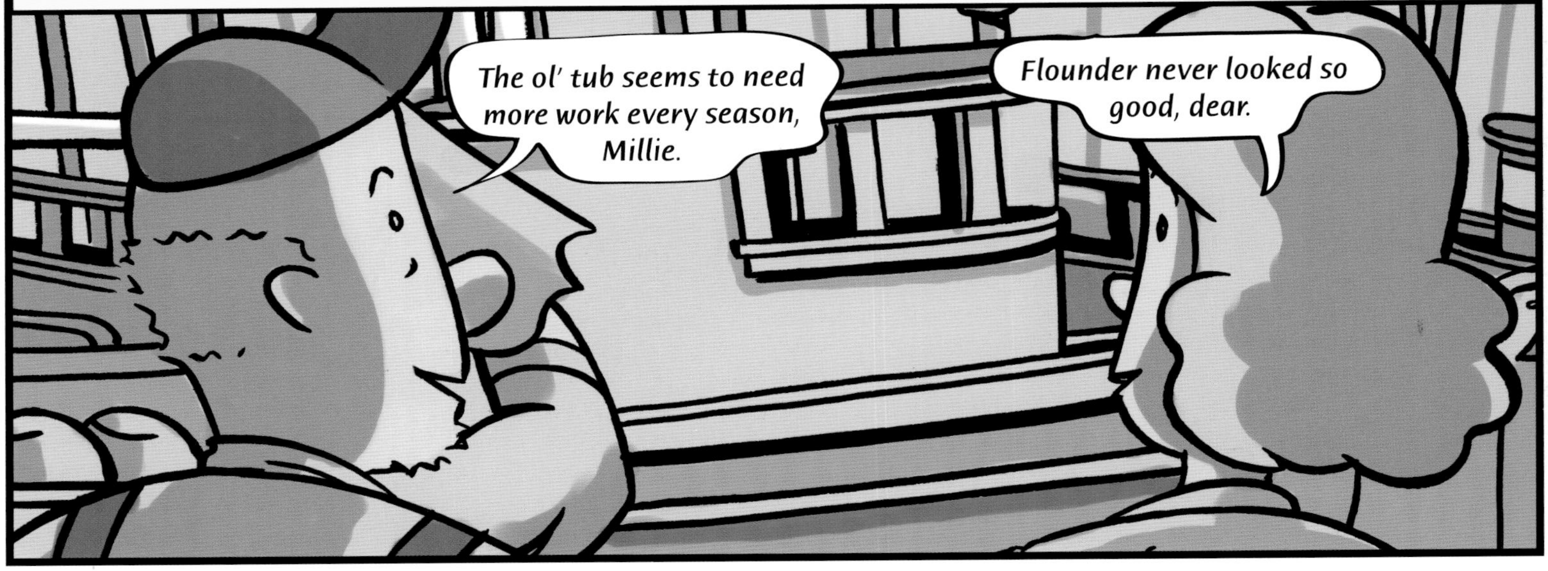

The ol' tub seems to need more work every season, Millie.
Flounder never looked so good, dear.

The salmon season opens soon and Gubby takes the *Flounder* out for a test run, taking along Millie and some friends for a bit of sport fishing.

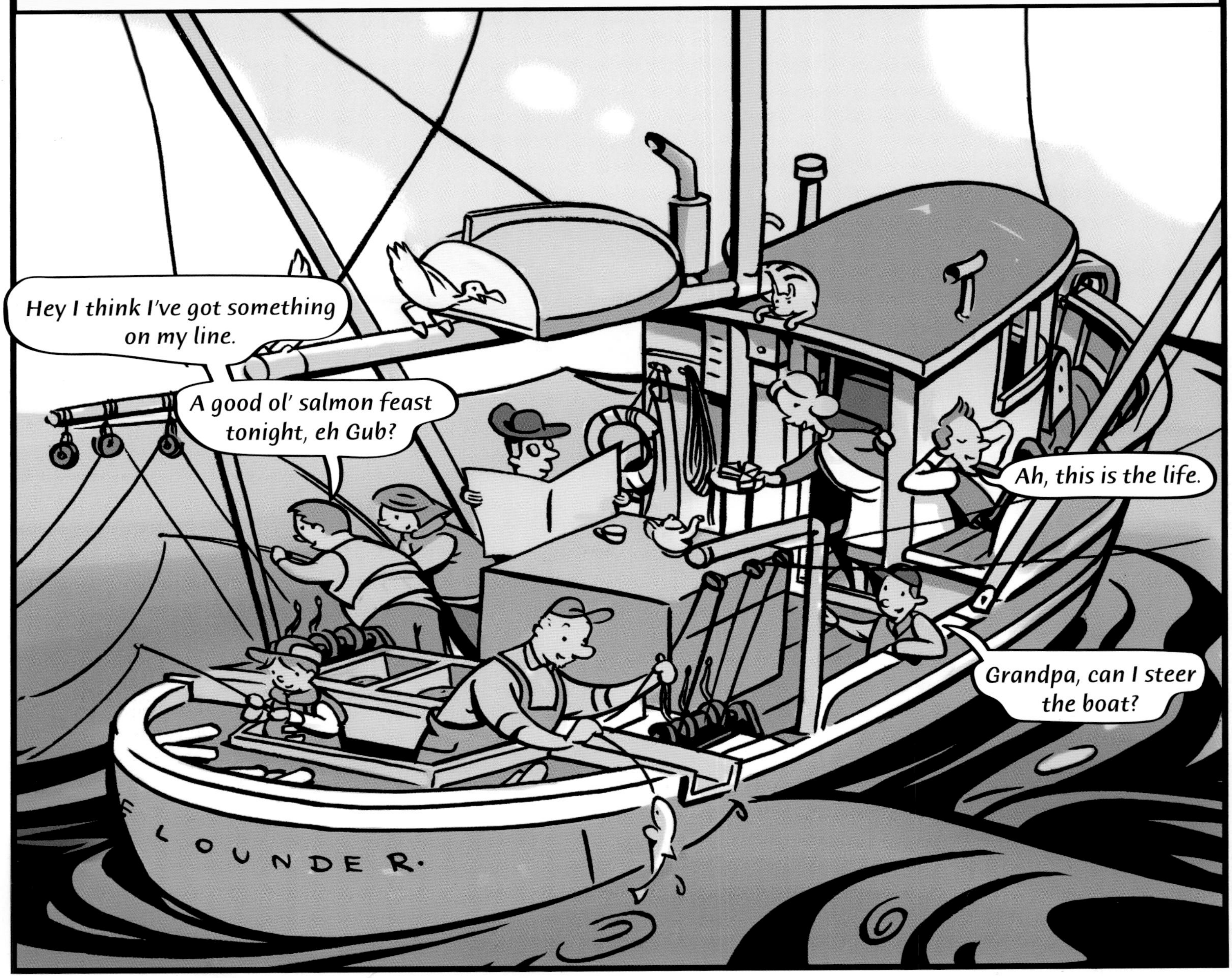

Hey I think I've got something on my line.
A good ol' salmon feast tonight, eh Gub?
Ah, this is the life.
Grandpa, can I steer the boat?

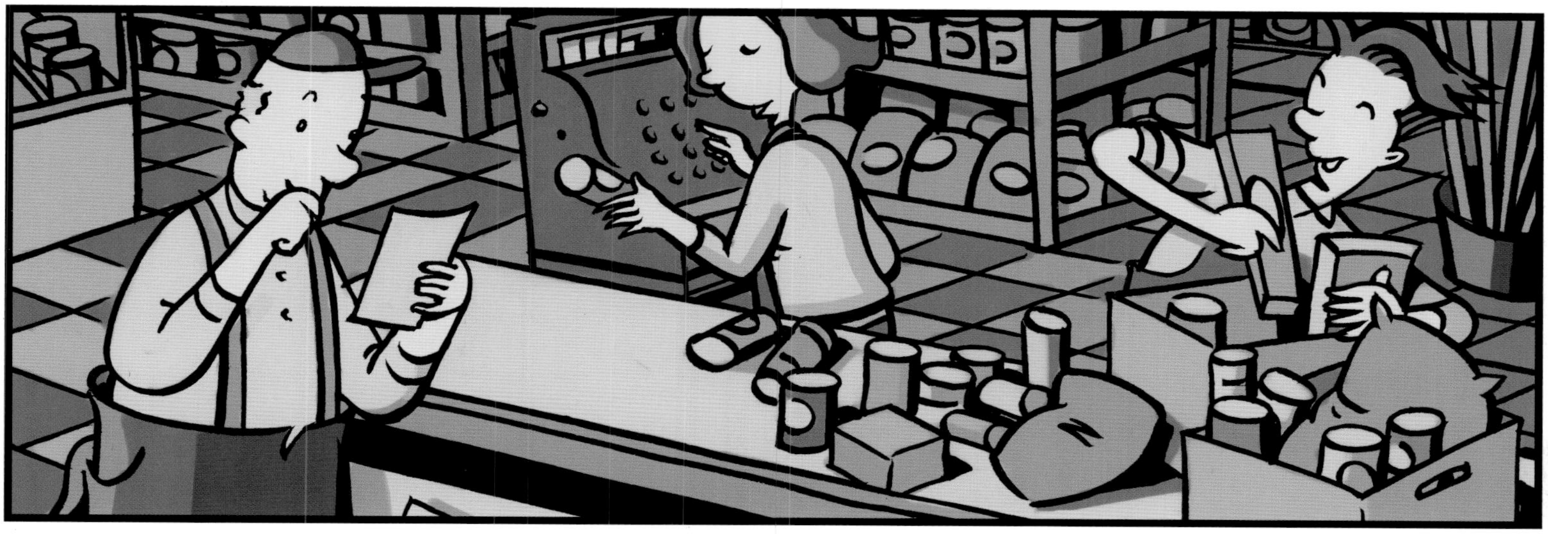

Before heading off on their big adventure Millie helps Gubby do some grocery shopping. She wants to make sure that he will have more to eat than beans on toast and orange pekoe tea, his favourite meal. Puss of course must have a very good supply of his Kitty Surprise cat food.

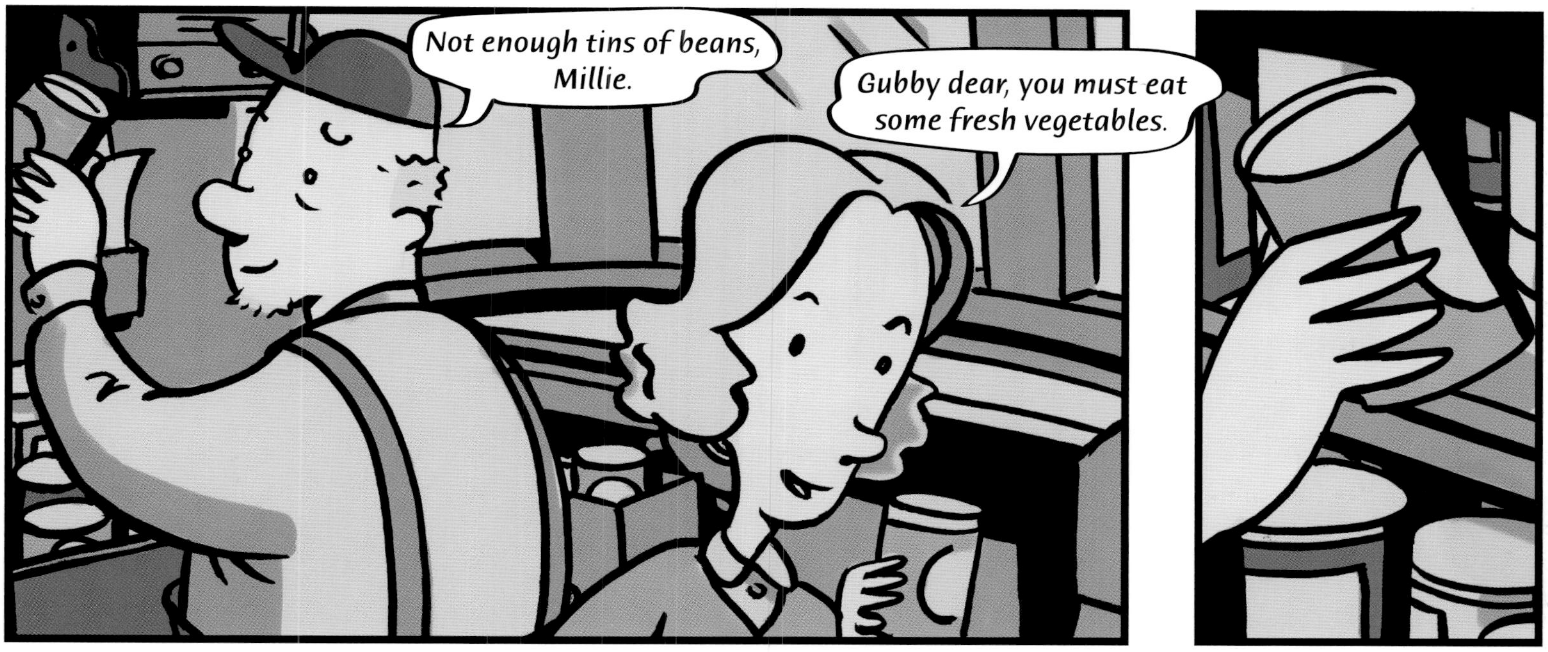

Not enough tins of beans, Millie.
Gubby dear, you must eat some fresh vegetables.

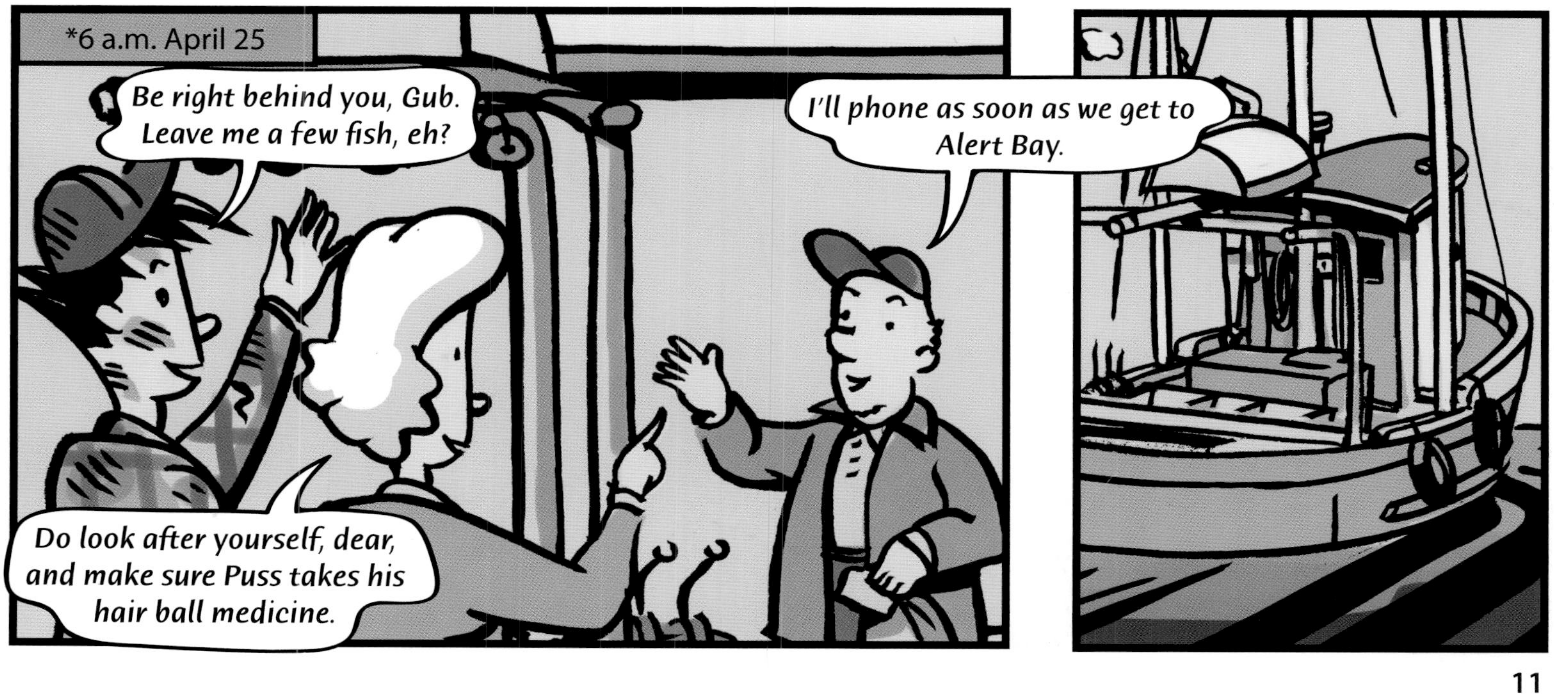

*6 a.m. April 25
Be right behind you, Gub. Leave me a few fish, eh?
I'll phone as soon as we get to Alert Bay.
Do look after yourself, dear, and make sure Puss takes his hair ball medicine.

*7 p.m.

After a very long day of travelling, the *Flounder* and its crew reach Stuart Island, which is at the top of the Strait of Georgia. This is the last stop before heading through many rapids, some of which can be dangerous for small boats.

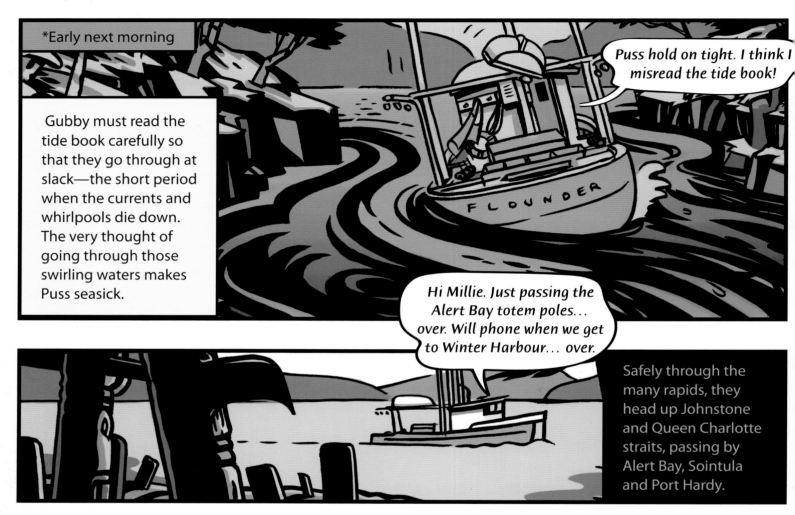

*Early next morning

Gubby must read the tide book carefully so that they go through at slack—the short period when the currents and whirlpools die down. The very thought of going through those swirling waters makes Puss seasick.

Puss hold on tight. I think I misread the tide book!

Hi Millie. Just passing the Alert Bay totem poles… over. Will phone when we get to Winter Harbour… over.

Safely through the many rapids, they head up Johnstone and Queen Charlotte straits, passing by Alert Bay, Sointula and Port Hardy.

*Later that day

Crikey, look at all those tubs, Puss. Looks like most of the trollers on the coast are here!

Finally they reach Bull Harbour where they will stay for the night. The harbour is full of fishing boats of every size and shape, all waiting for good weather before heading to the many fishing grounds. Some boats even go as far north as the Queen Charlotte Islands.

12

Fishboats come in many sizes. The *Skookumchuck* is 48 feet (16 metres) long and has four crew members. It has a large freezer to keep fish from spoiling and can stay out on the fishing grounds for a long time. The *Flounder's* fish are kept cool with ice and last only a few days before Gubby must bring them into the harbour.

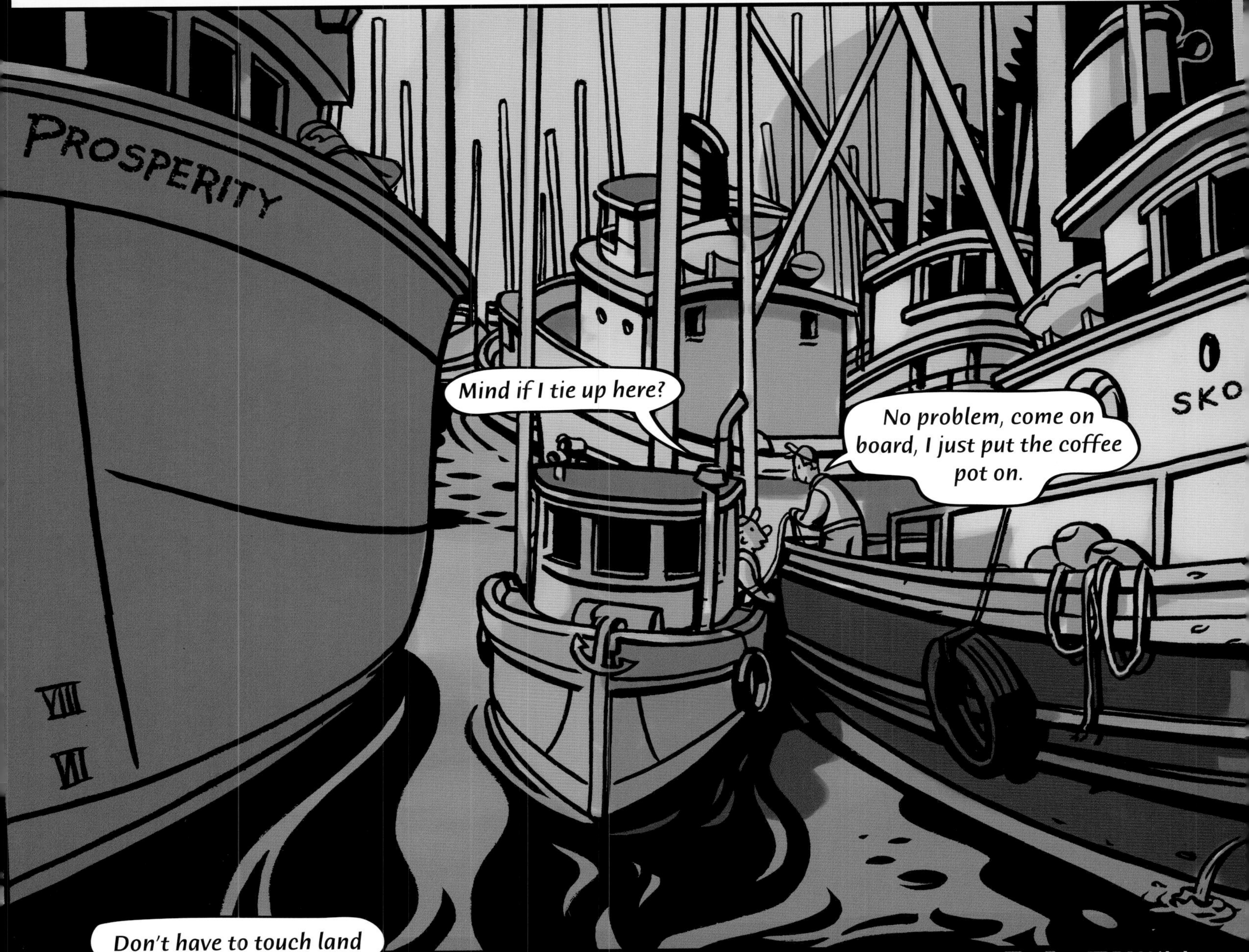

PROSPERITY
Mind if I tie up here?
No problem, come on board, I just put the coffee pot on.
SKO

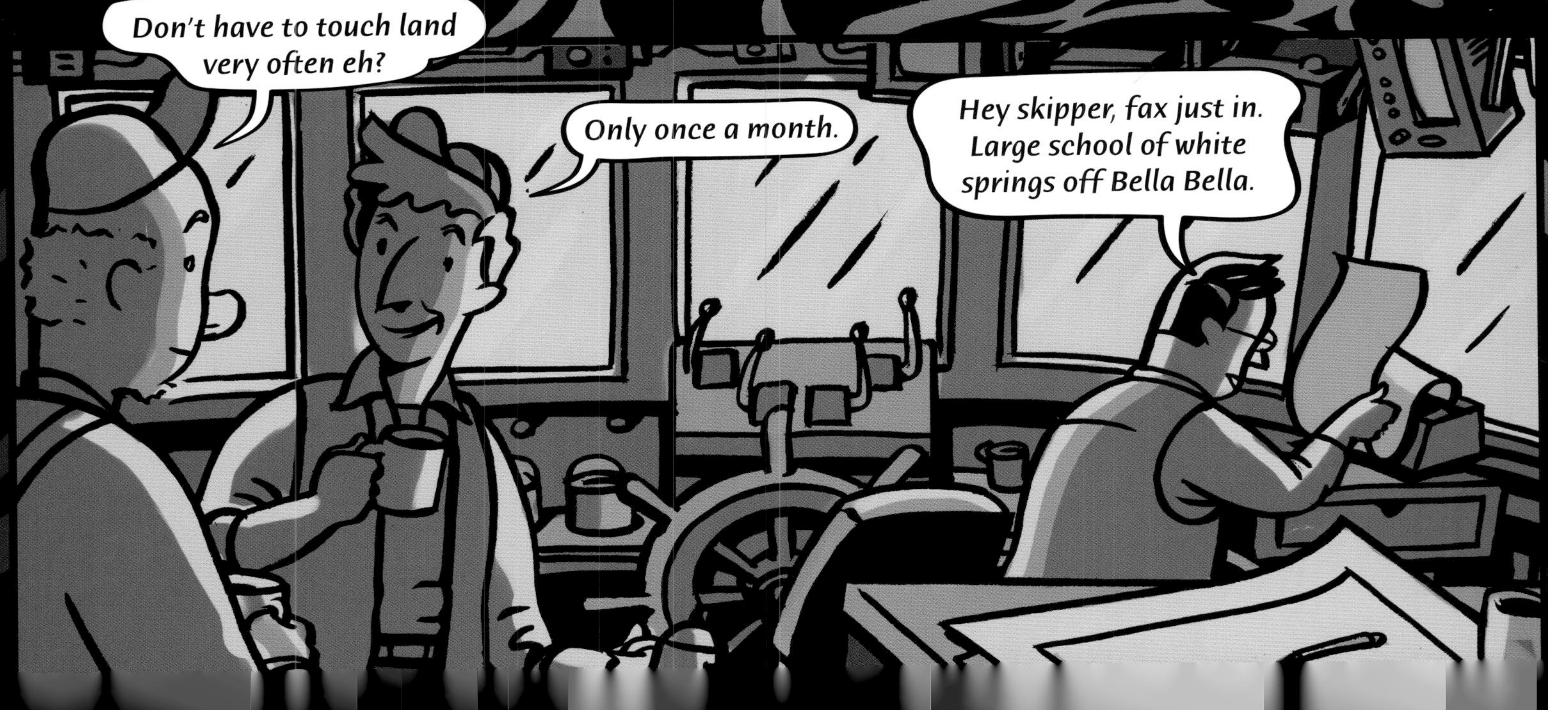

Don't have to touch land very often eh?
Only once a month.
Hey skipper, fax just in. Large school of white springs off Bella Bella.

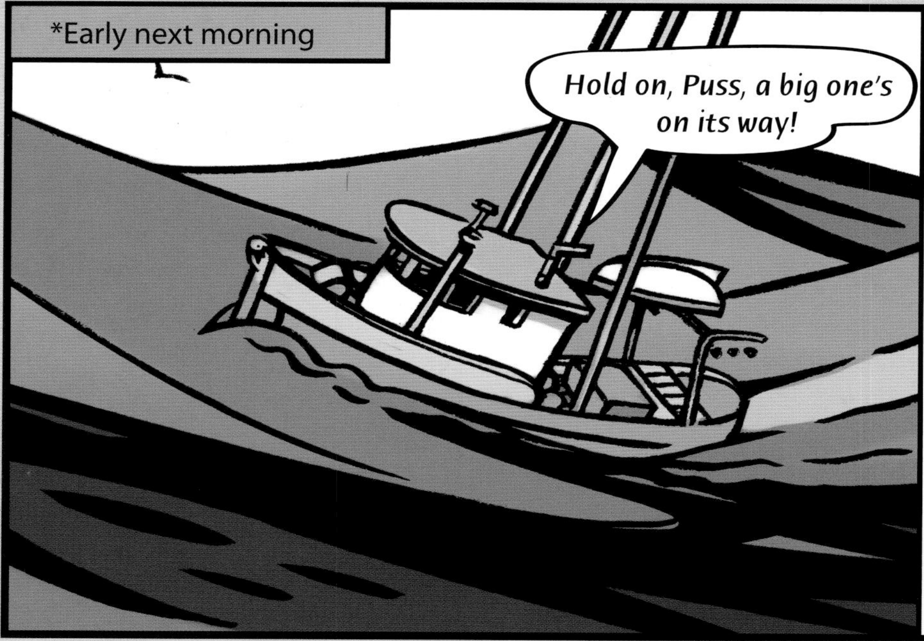
*Early next morning
Hold on, Puss, a big one's on its way!

The *Flounder* slips away from Bull Harbour and crosses dangerous Nahwitti Bar, then heads into the open ocean off Cape Scott. The cape sometimes has great waves that could sink a small boat like the *Flounder* and Gubby and Puss grit their teeth as they head toward the churning seas. Just as they think they are through the worst of it a giant wave rolls over the *Flounder*'s deck and washes away Gubby's new crab trap. Puss is terrified but they are through the roughest part and are safely on their way down the west coast of Vancouver Island.

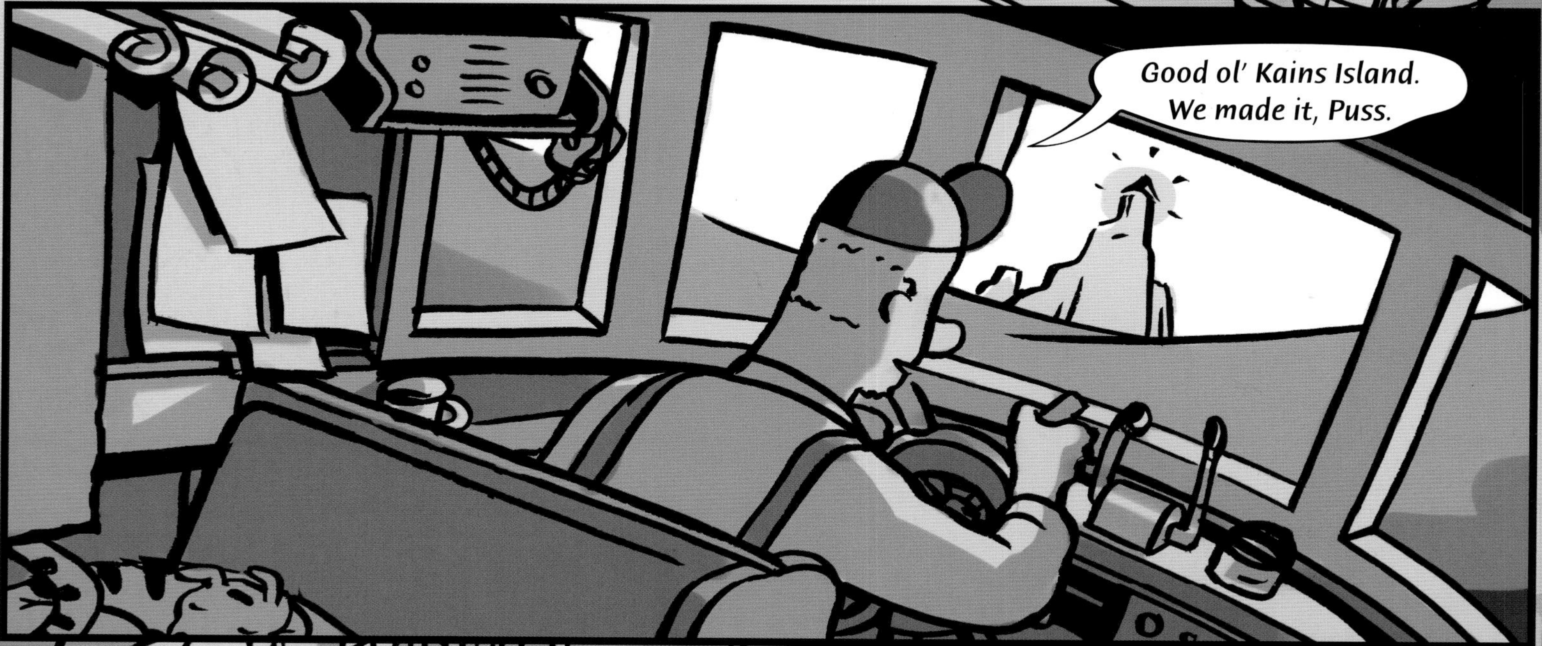
Good ol' Kains Island. We made it, Puss.

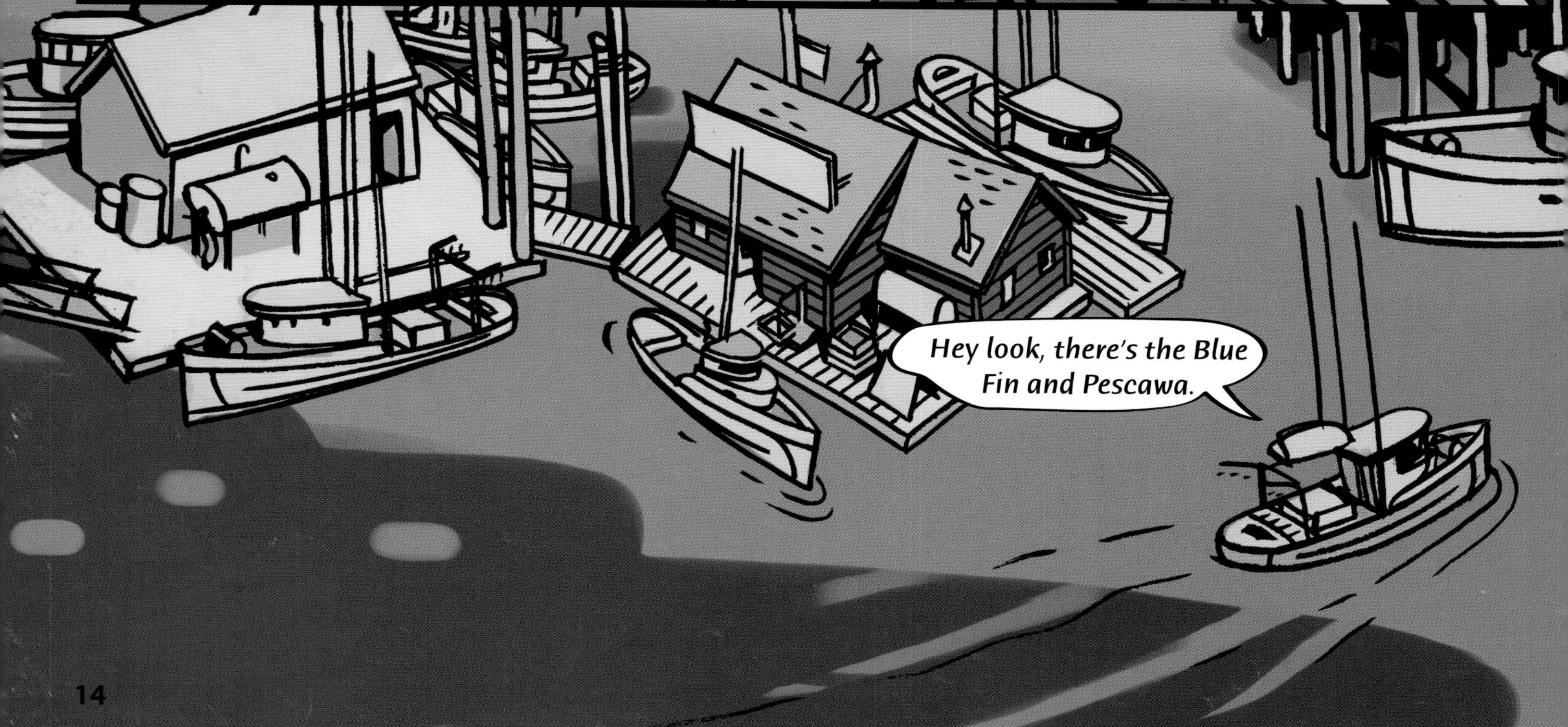
Hey look, there's the Blue Fin and Pescawa.

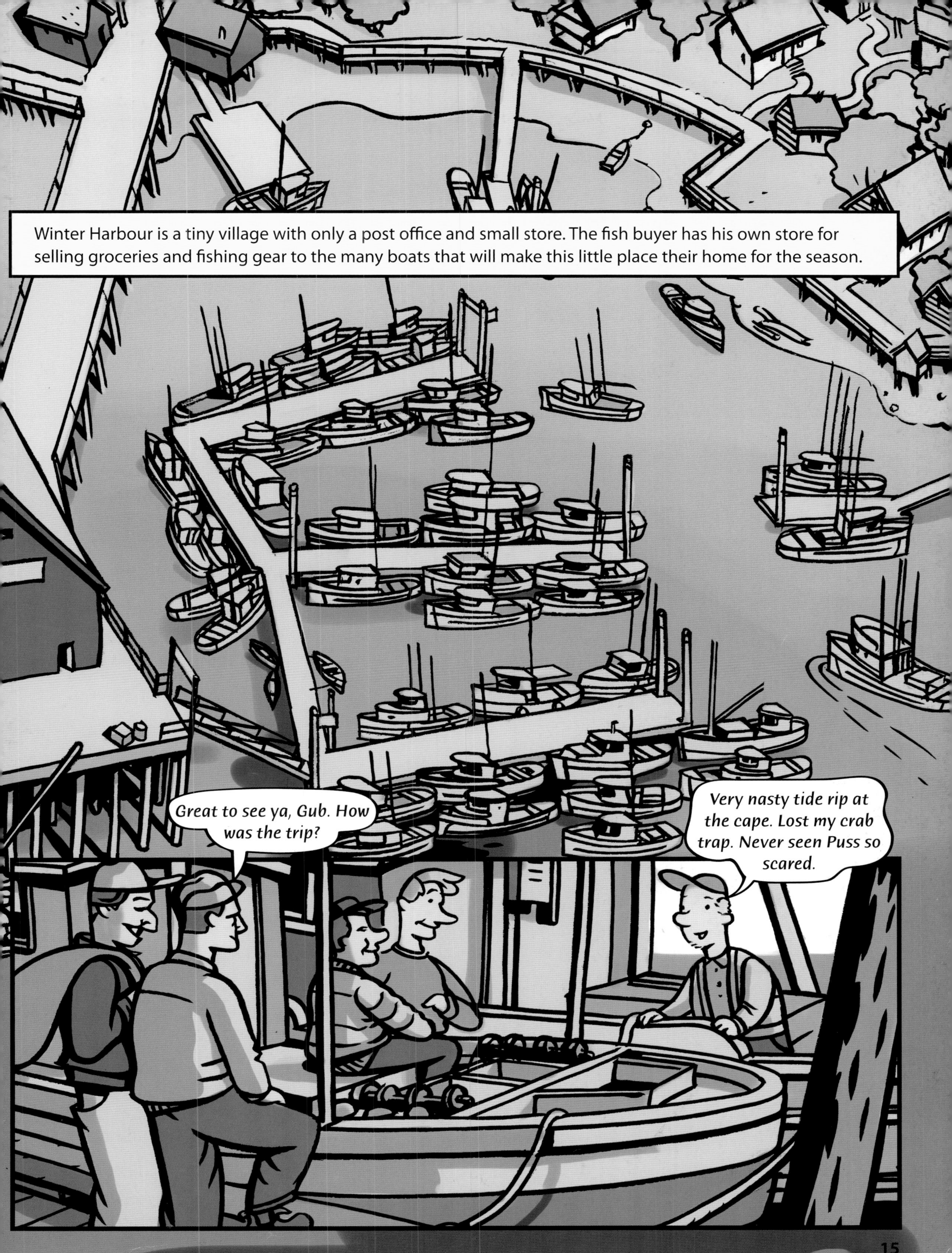
Winter Harbour is a tiny village with only a post office and small store. The fish buyer has his own store for selling groceries and fishing gear to the many boats that will make this little place their home for the season.
Great to see ya, Gub. How was the trip?
Very nasty tide rip at the cape. Lost my crab trap. Never seen Puss so scared.

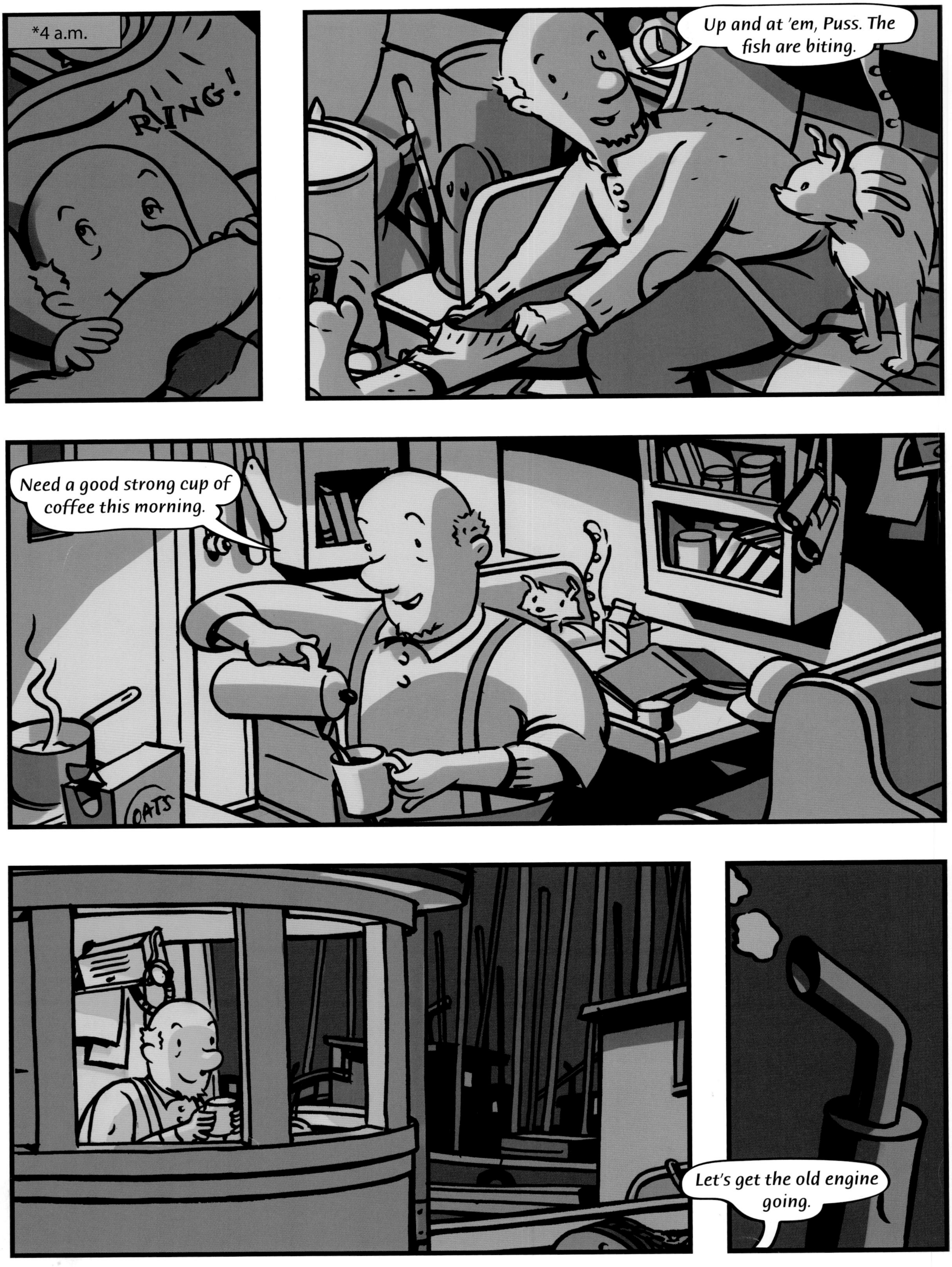
*4 a.m.
RING!
Up and at 'em, Puss. The fish are biting.
Need a good strong cup of coffee this morning.
OATS
Let's get the old engine going.

It's cold and dark at four in the morning and some of the fishermen are quite happy to sleep just a little longer in their snug little berths.

Can't catch fish at the wharf.

Hell's bells, Gub, the fish are still in their beds!

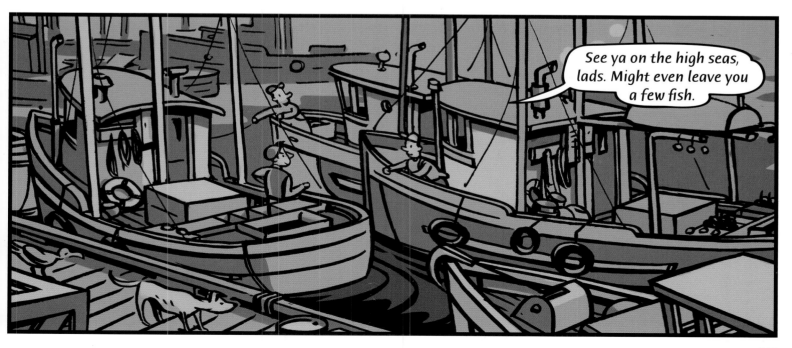

See ya on the high seas, lads. Might even leave you a few fish.

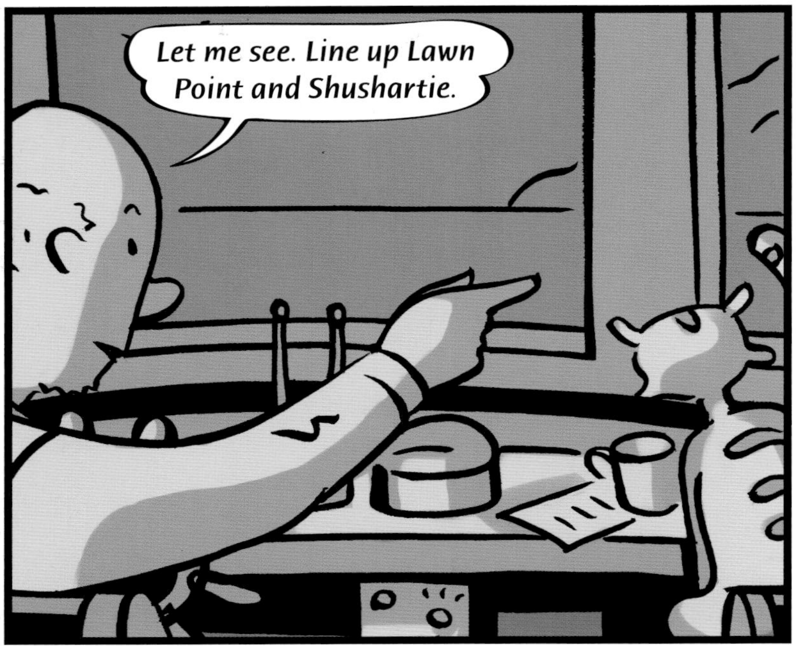
Let me see. Line up Lawn Point and Shushartie.

The first trip out into the open ocean is a little scary, even for Gubby. The waves crashing against the shore are gigantic. But he can hardly wait to get to his favourite fishing spots.

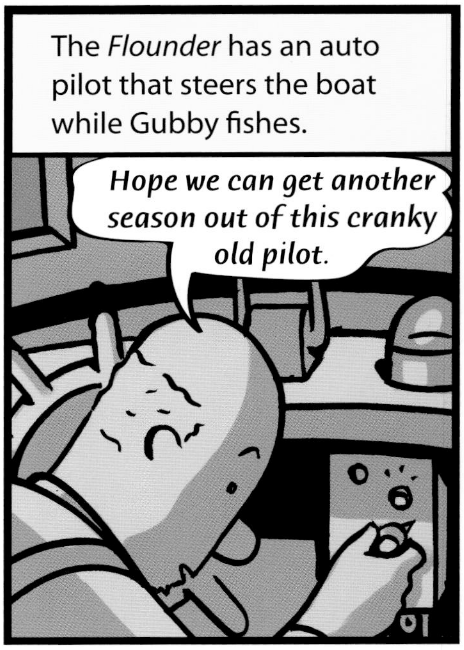
The *Flounder* has an auto pilot that steers the boat while Gubby fishes.
Hope we can get another season out of this cranky old pilot.

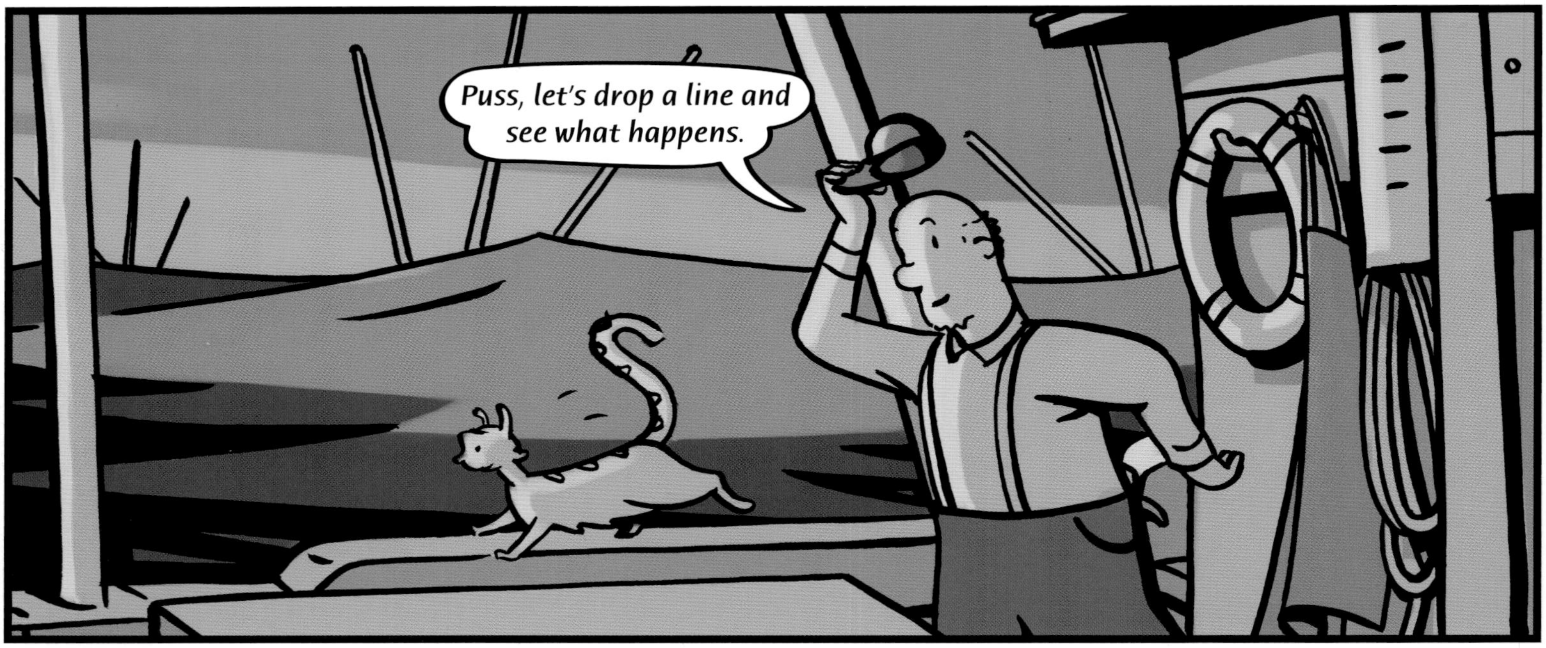
Puss, let's drop a line and see what happens.

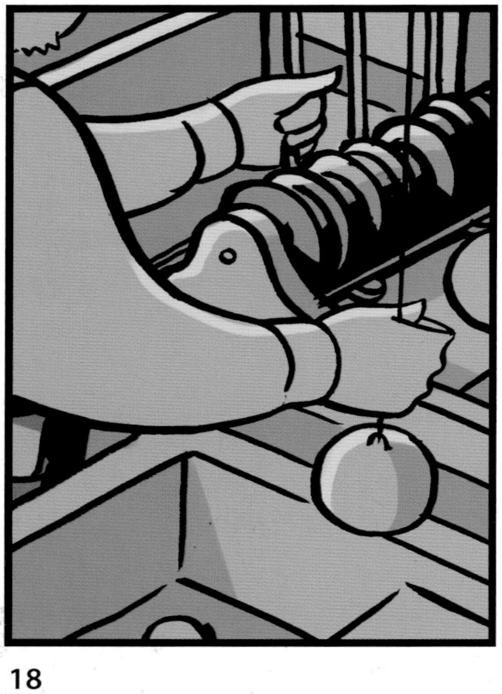

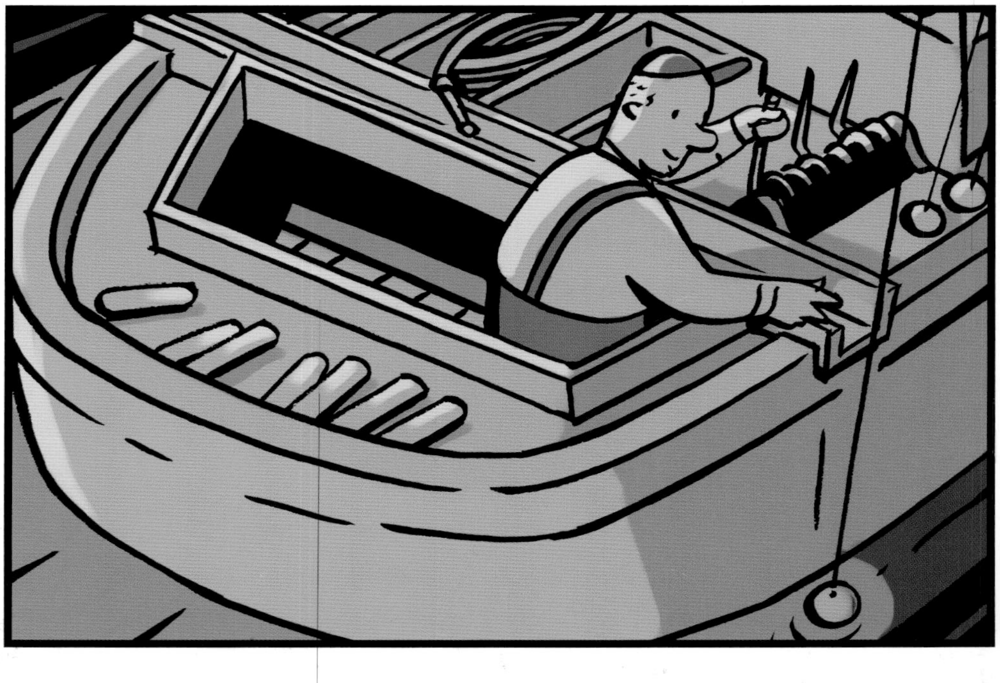

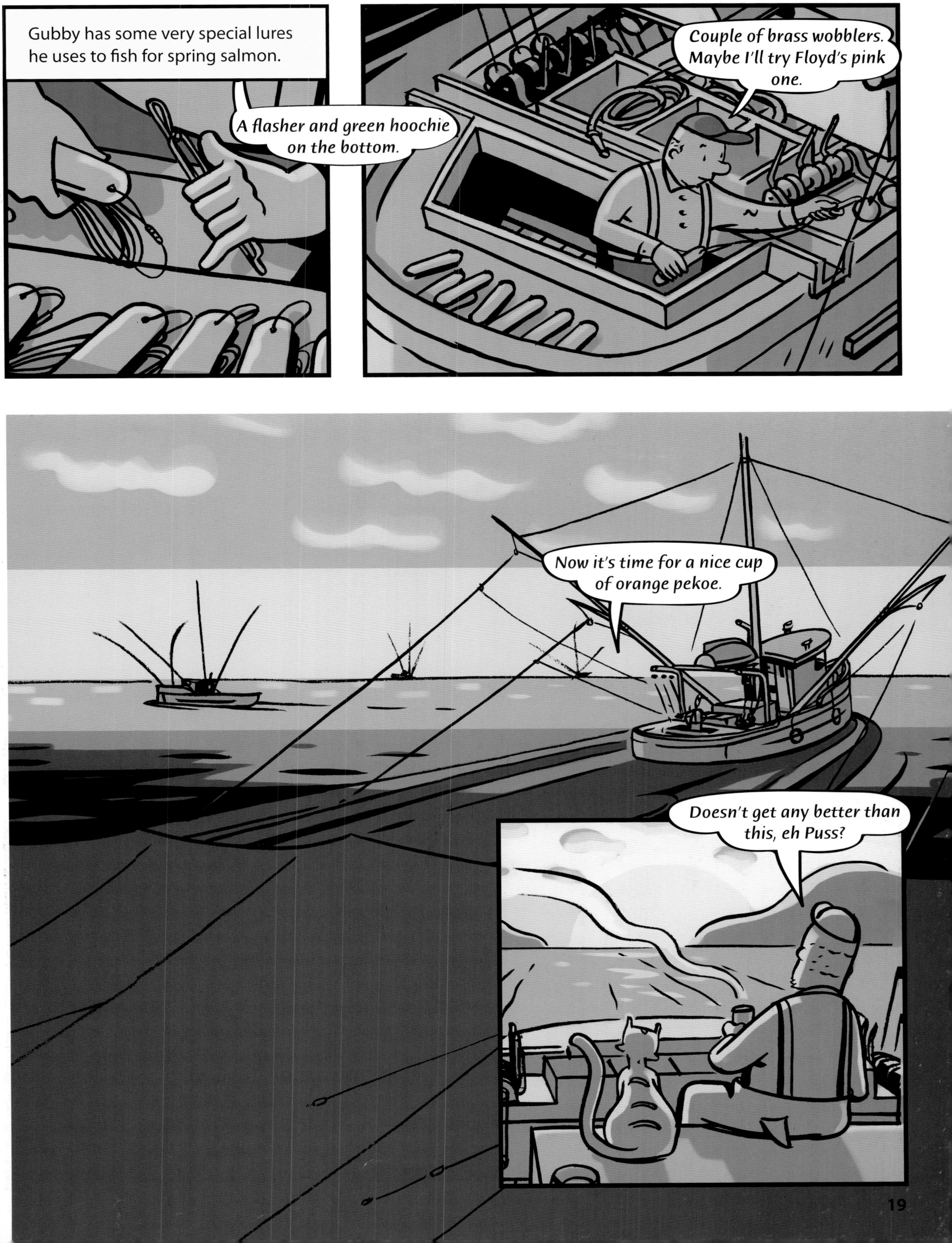
Gubby has some very special lures he uses to fish for spring salmon.
A flasher and green hoochie on the bottom.
Couple of brass wobblers. Maybe I'll try Floyd's pink one.
Now it's time for a nice cup of orange pekoe.
Doesn't get any better than this, eh Puss?

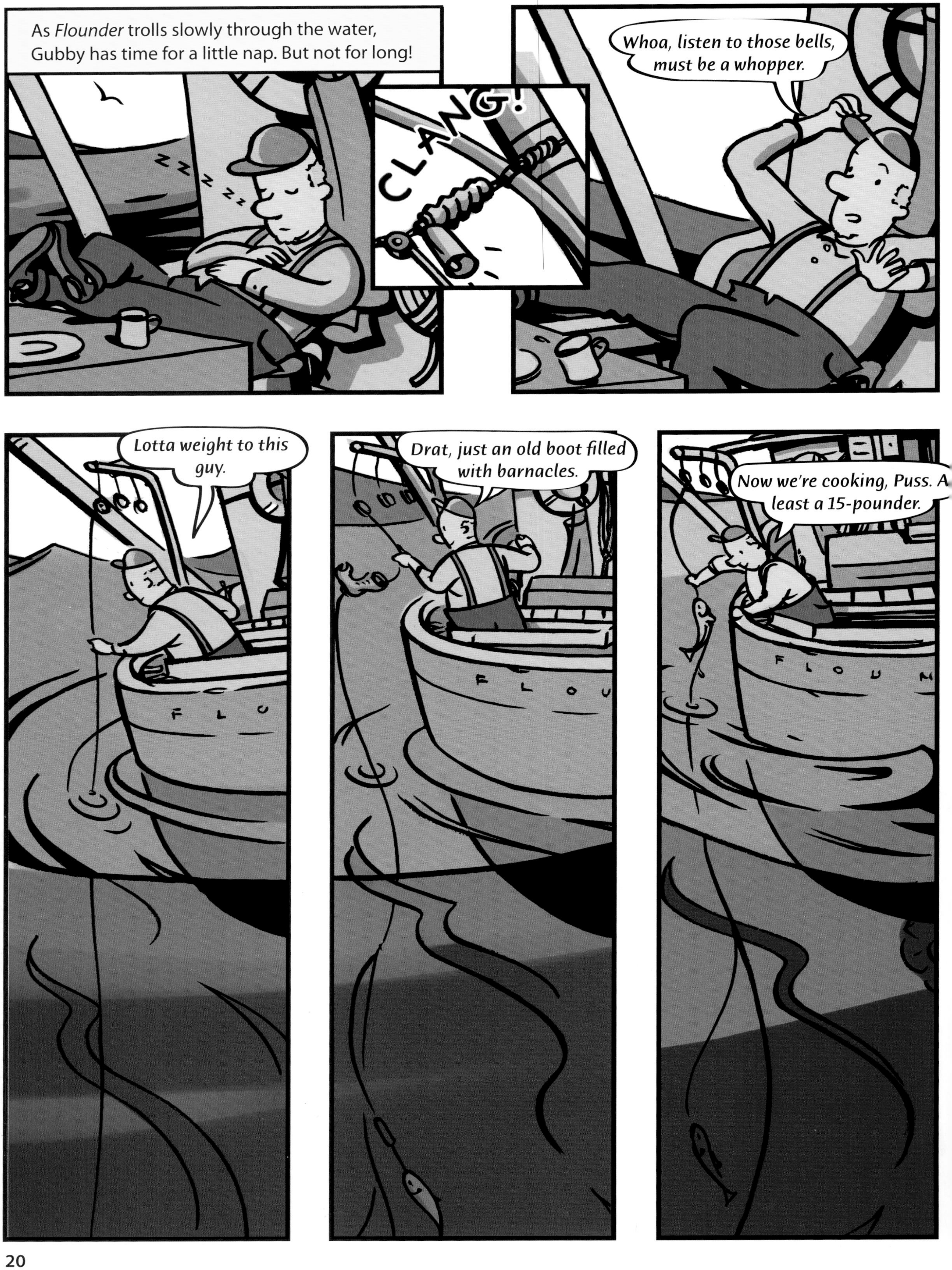
As *Flounder* trolls slowly through the water, Gubby has time for a little nap. But not for long!
CLANG!
Whoa, listen to those bells, must be a whopper.
Lotta weight to this guy.
Drat, just an old boot filled with barnacles.
Now we're cooking, Puss. A least a 15-pounder.

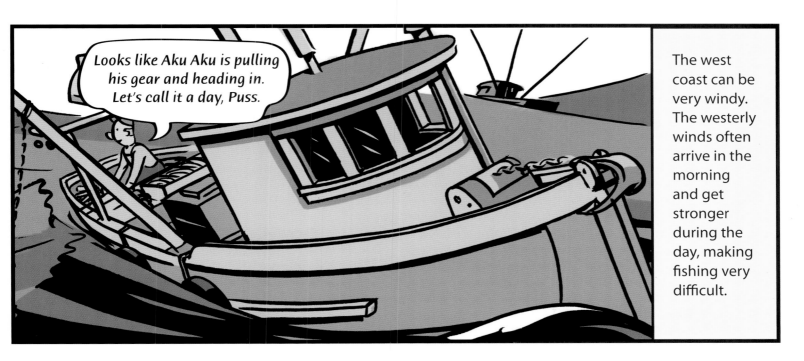

Looks like Aku Aku is pulling his gear and heading in. Let's call it a day, Puss.

The west coast can be very windy. The westerly winds often arrive in the morning and get stronger during the day, making fishing very difficult.

Many boats are lined up to sell their fish to Big Louie, the fish buyer.

PACKERS
Louie PROP.

Spring salmon all look the same on the outside, but inside their flesh is tinted either reddish or whitish. White ones are just as good but sell for much less. Gubby grumbles about this but knows that people in the city like their salmon red.

Pretty good haul, Gub. It's been a good spring salmon season so far.

WHITES .29 ¢
REDS $ 1.29

I'm afraid they're all whites.

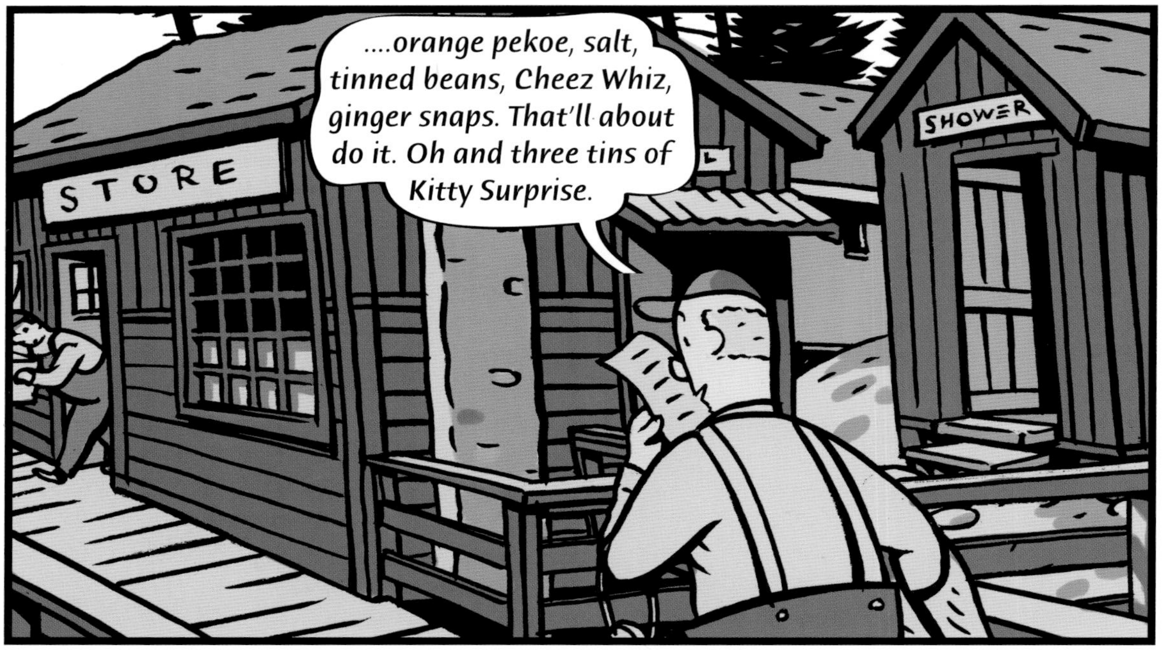
STORE
SHOWER
....orange pekoe, salt, tinned beans, Cheez Whiz, ginger snaps. That'll about do it. Oh and three tins of Kitty Surprise.

Spring salmon fishing is leisurely compared to the coho season, when fish arrive in great bunches or schools. The fishermen must have their special hoochies and wobblers ready, because the action is nonstop. In the meantime they fish for springs, do a little shopping and visit their pals on the wharf.

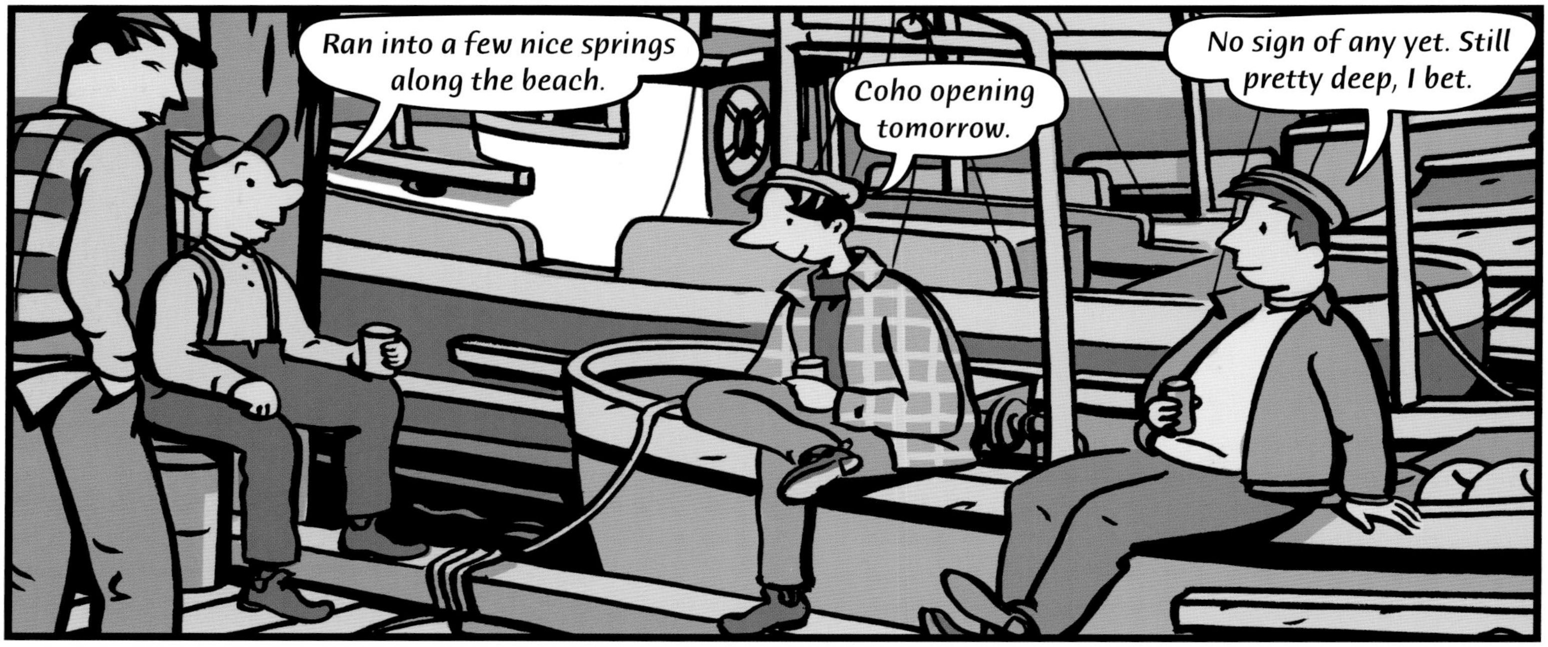
Ran into a few nice springs along the beach.
Coho opening tomorrow.
No sign of any yet. Still pretty deep, I bet.

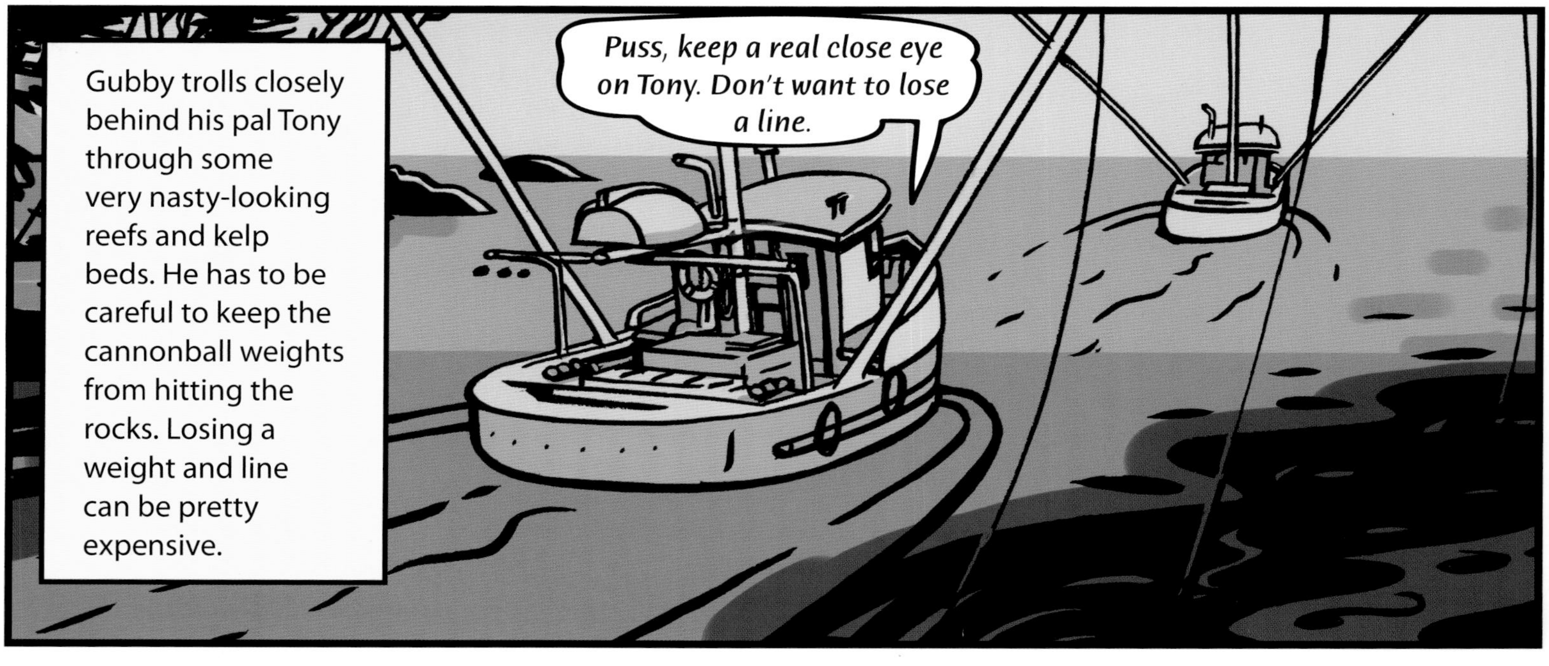
Gubby trolls closely behind his pal Tony through some very nasty-looking reefs and kelp beds. He has to be careful to keep the cannonball weights from hitting the rocks. Losing a weight and line can be pretty expensive.
Puss, keep a real close eye on Tony. Don't want to lose a line.

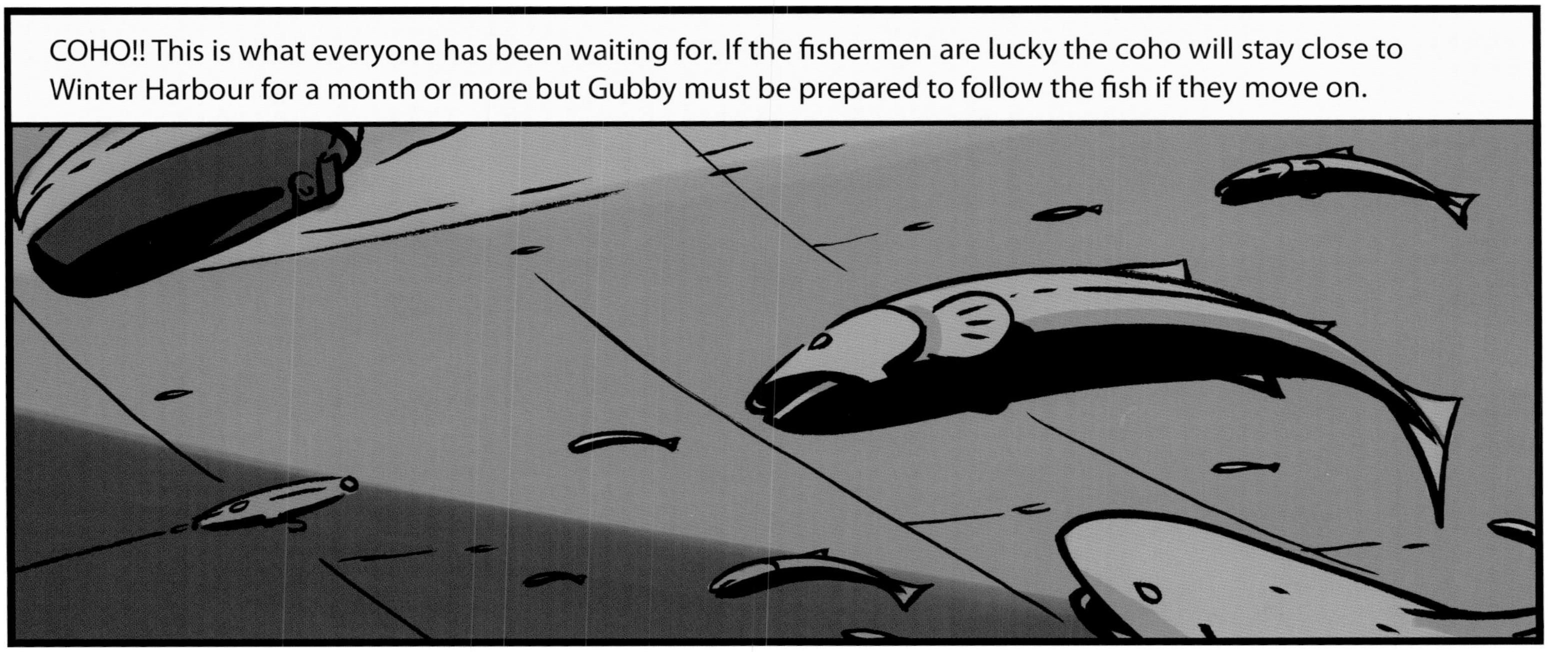
COHO!! This is what everyone has been waiting for. If the fishermen are lucky the coho will stay close to Winter Harbour for a month or more but Gubby must be prepared to follow the fish if they move on.

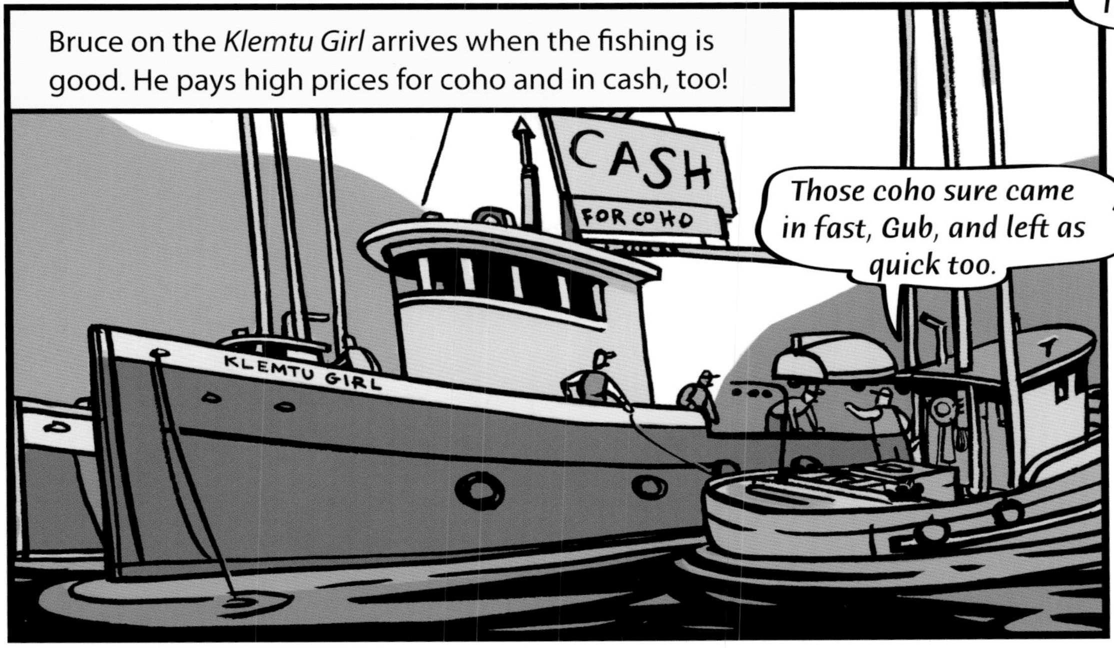
Bruce on the *Klemtu Girl* arrives when the fishing is good. He pays high prices for coho and in cash, too!
CASH
FOR COHO
KLEMTU GIRL
Those coho sure came in fast, Gub, and left as quick too.

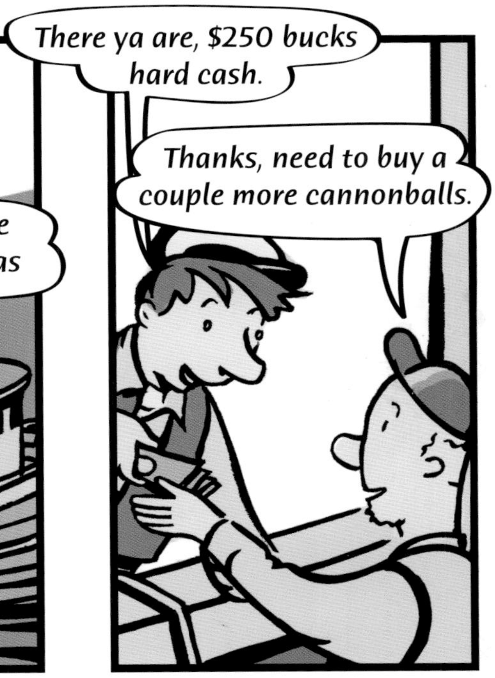
There ya are, $250 bucks hard cash.
Thanks, need to buy a couple more cannonballs.

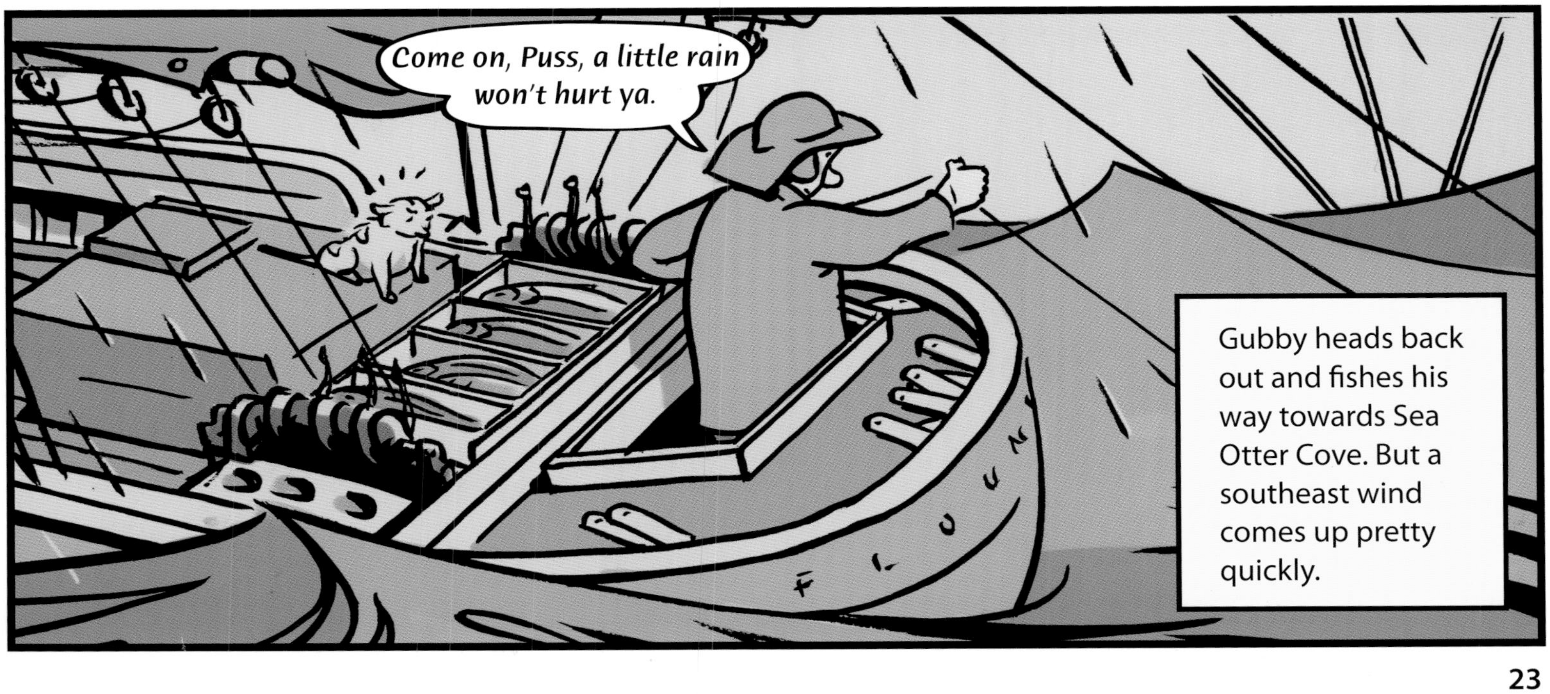
Come on, Puss, a little rain won't hurt ya.
Gubby heads back out and fishes his way towards Sea Otter Cove. But a southeast wind comes up pretty quickly.

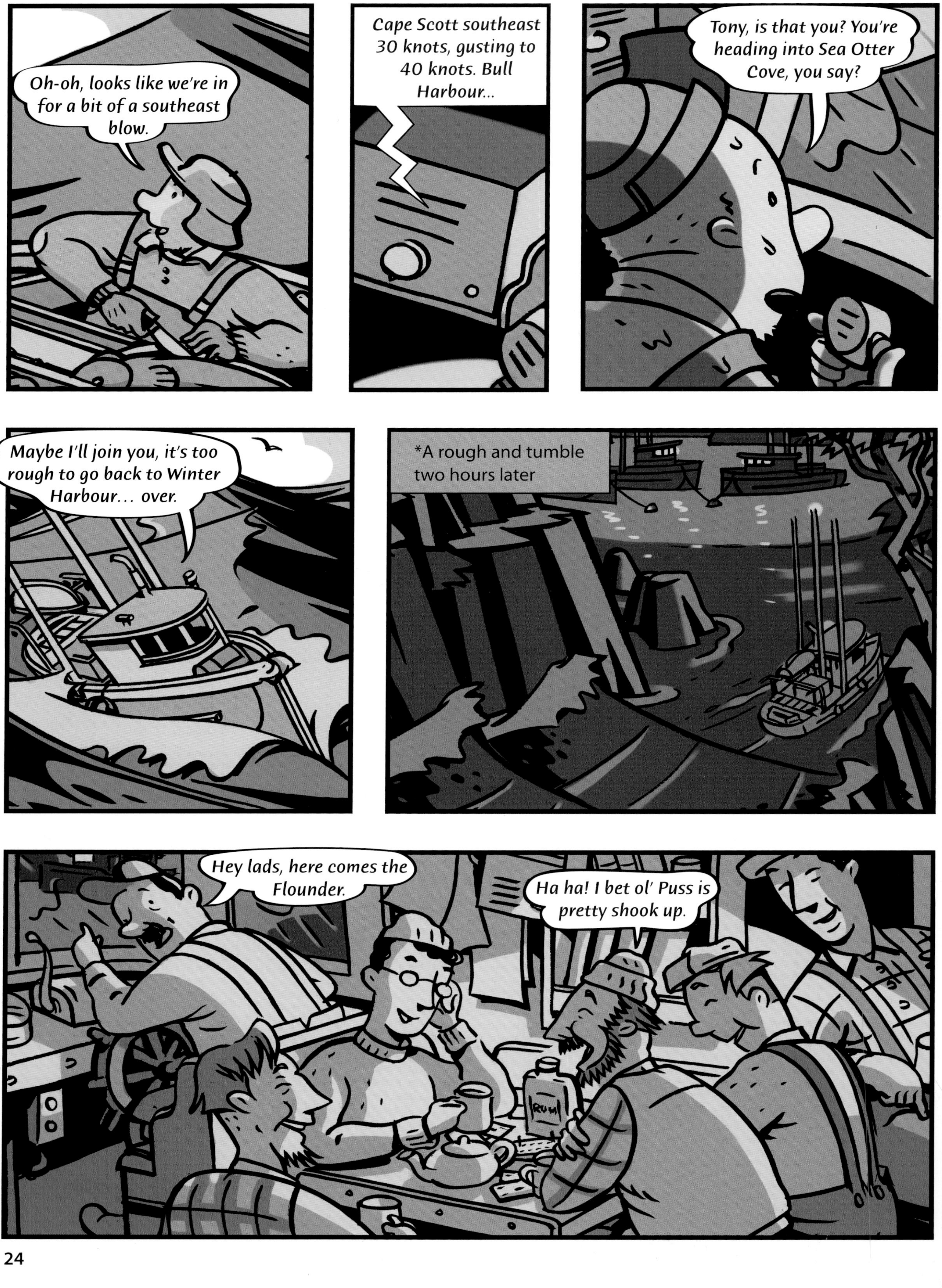
Oh-oh, looks like we're in for a bit of a southeast blow.
Cape Scott southeast 30 knots, gusting to 40 knots. Bull Harbour...
Tony, is that you? You're heading into Sea Otter Cove, you say?
Maybe I'll join you, it's too rough to go back to Winter Harbour... over.
*A rough and tumble two hours later
Hey lads, here comes the Flounder.
Ha ha! I bet ol' Puss is pretty shook up.
RUM

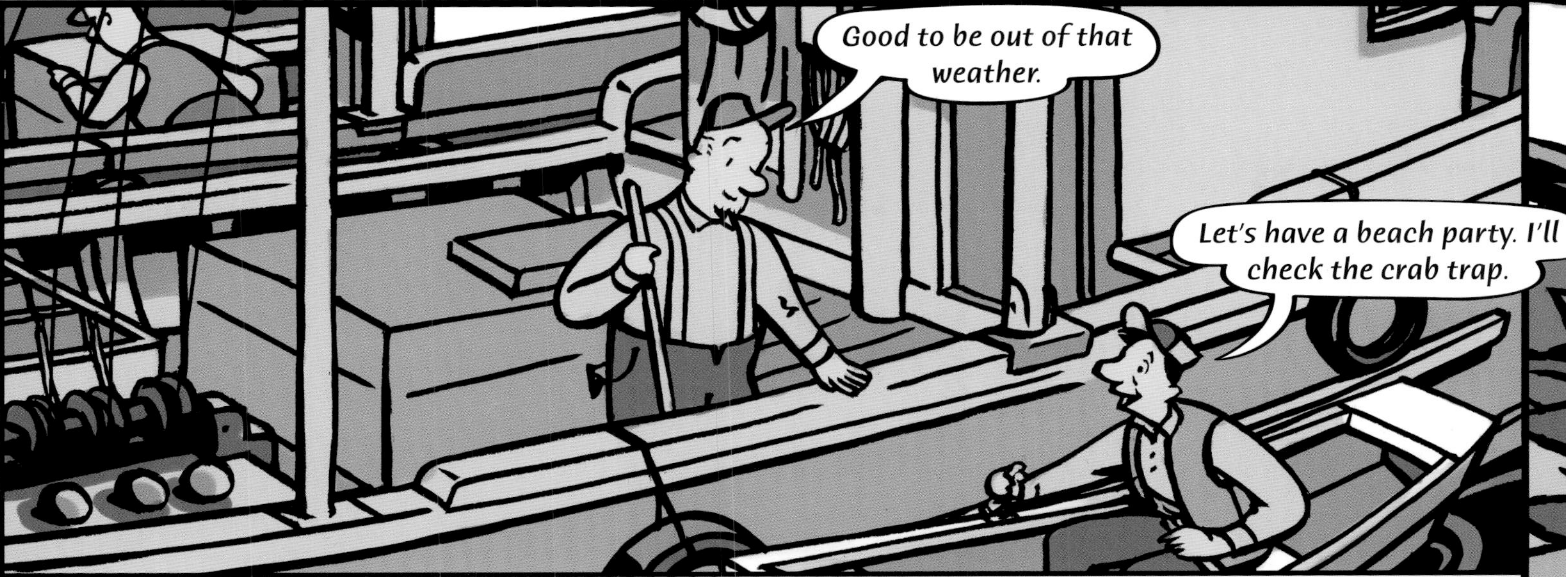
Good to be out of that weather.
Let's have a beach party. I'll check the crab trap.

Days when it's too stormy to fish are called "harbour days." They can be quite a treat after many long days of fishing. There is time for napping, reading and playing cards. Some boats need repairs after being damaged by the storm. And there is always time for a beach barbecue. What could be more fun? Gubby has a small halibut and Reg and Mel have crab and prawn traps. It's going to be a feast!

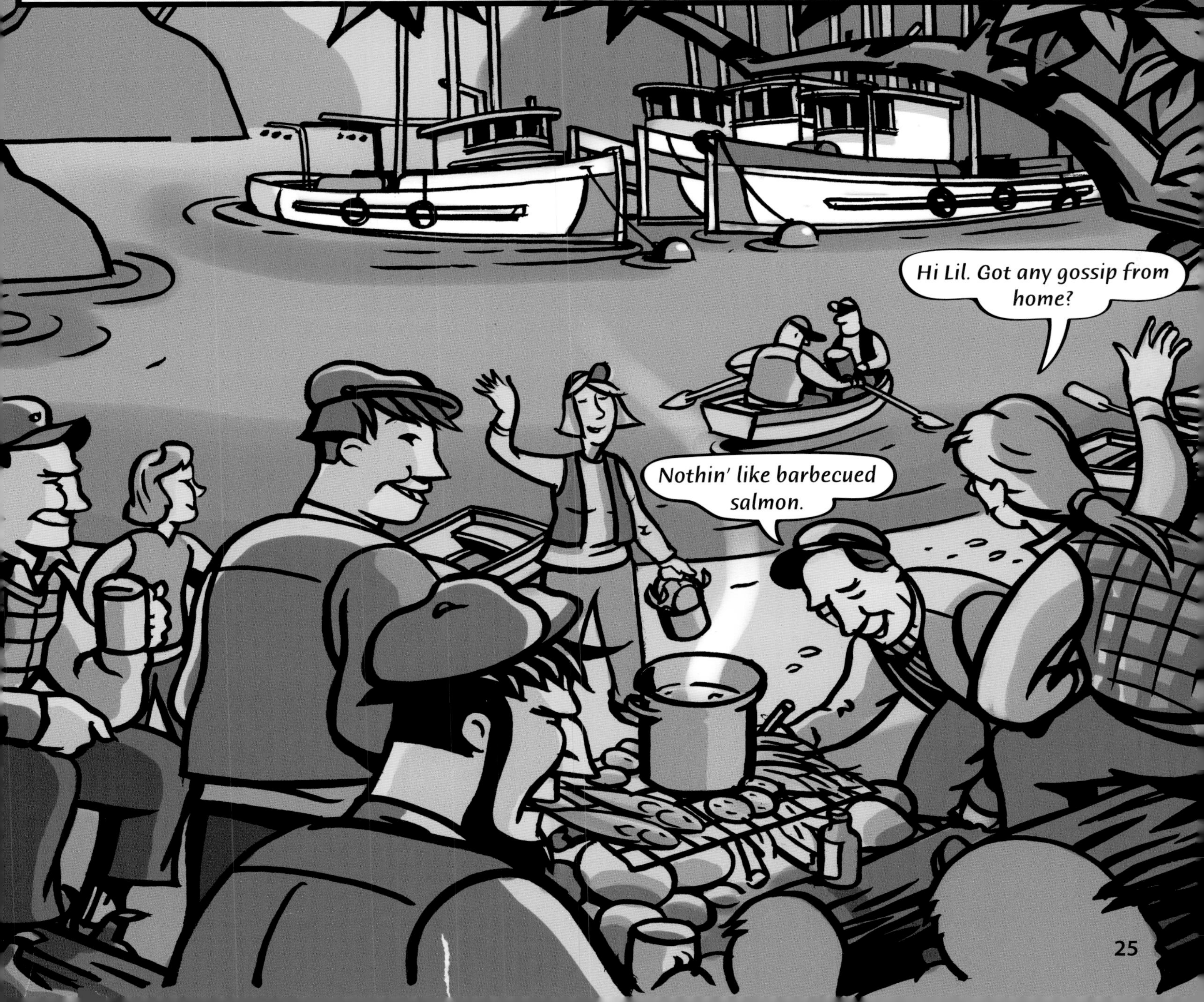
Hi Lil. Got any gossip from home?
Nothin' like barbecued salmon.

After a few days it is time to fish again. The storm stirs up the ocean so much that the fish disappear and the fleet must decide where to find them. Gubby is in no hurry and is content to troll back to Winter Harbour.

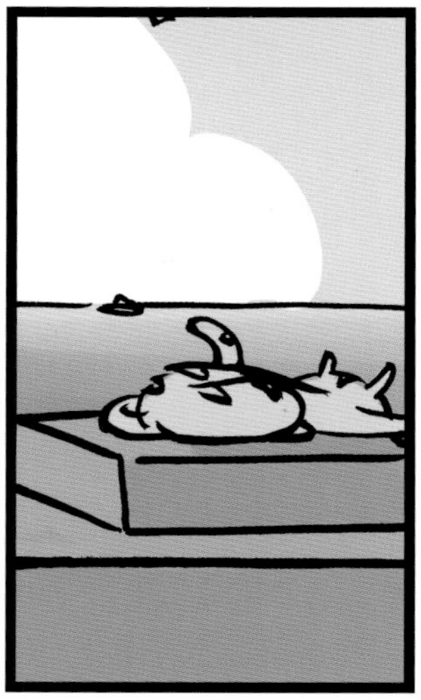

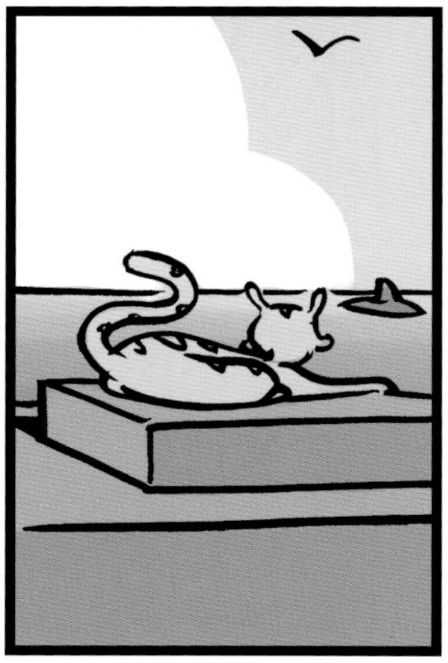

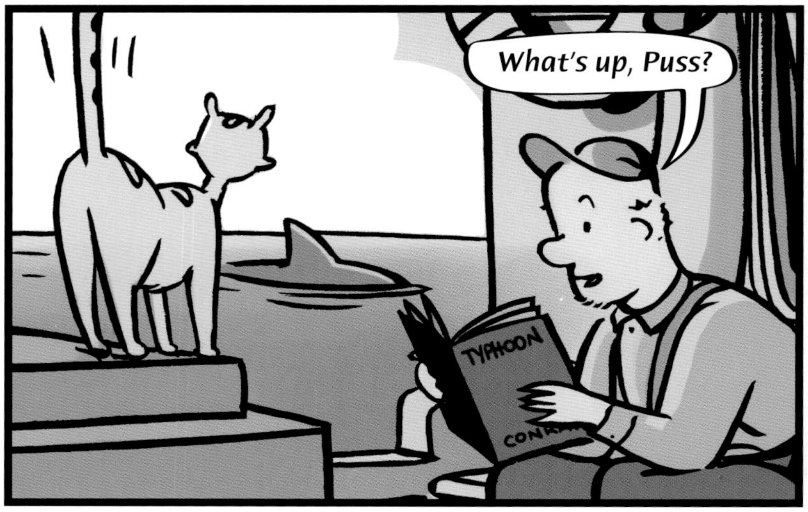
What's up, Puss?
TYPHOON

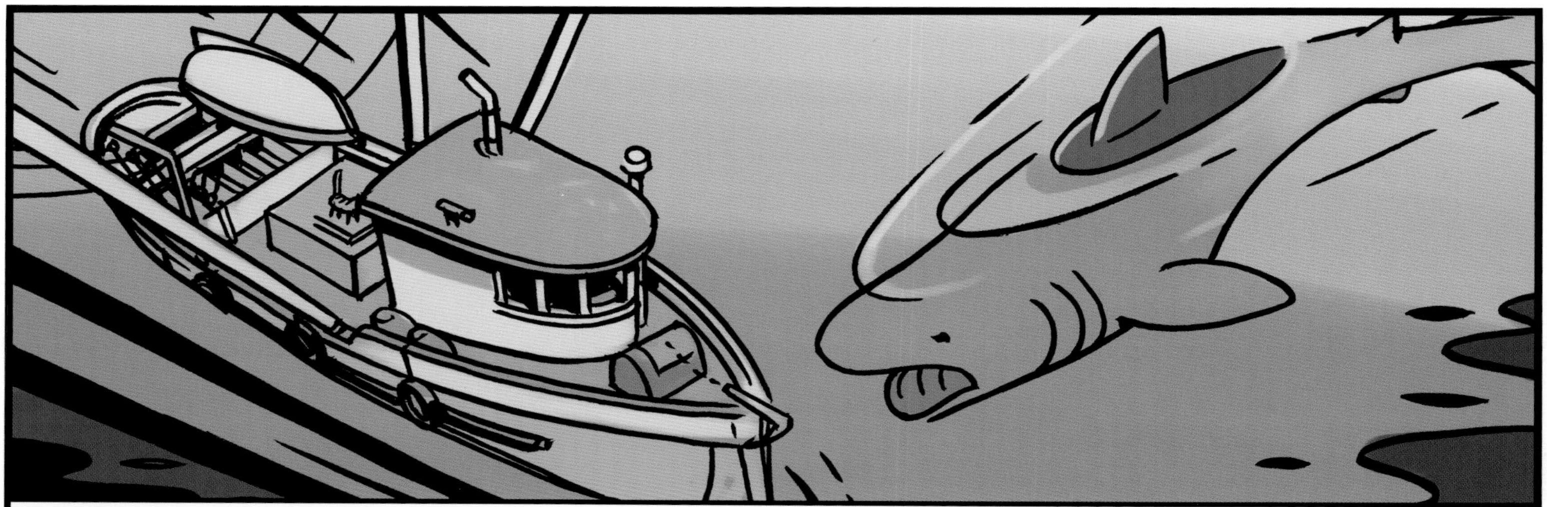

What Puss saw was a basking shark, one of the largest fish in the ocean. They do not have sharp teeth like some sharks but can be dangerous if startled while dozing near the surface.

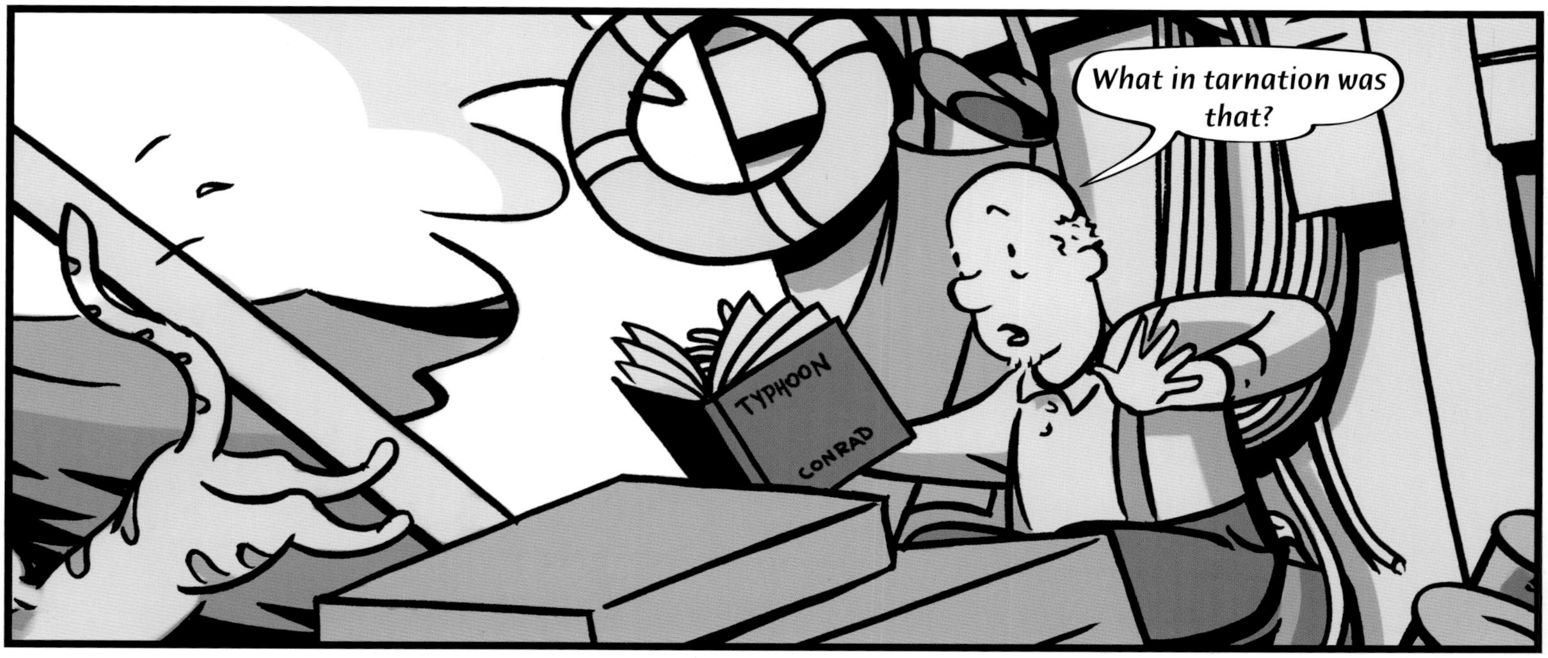
What in tarnation was that?
TYPHOON
CONRAD

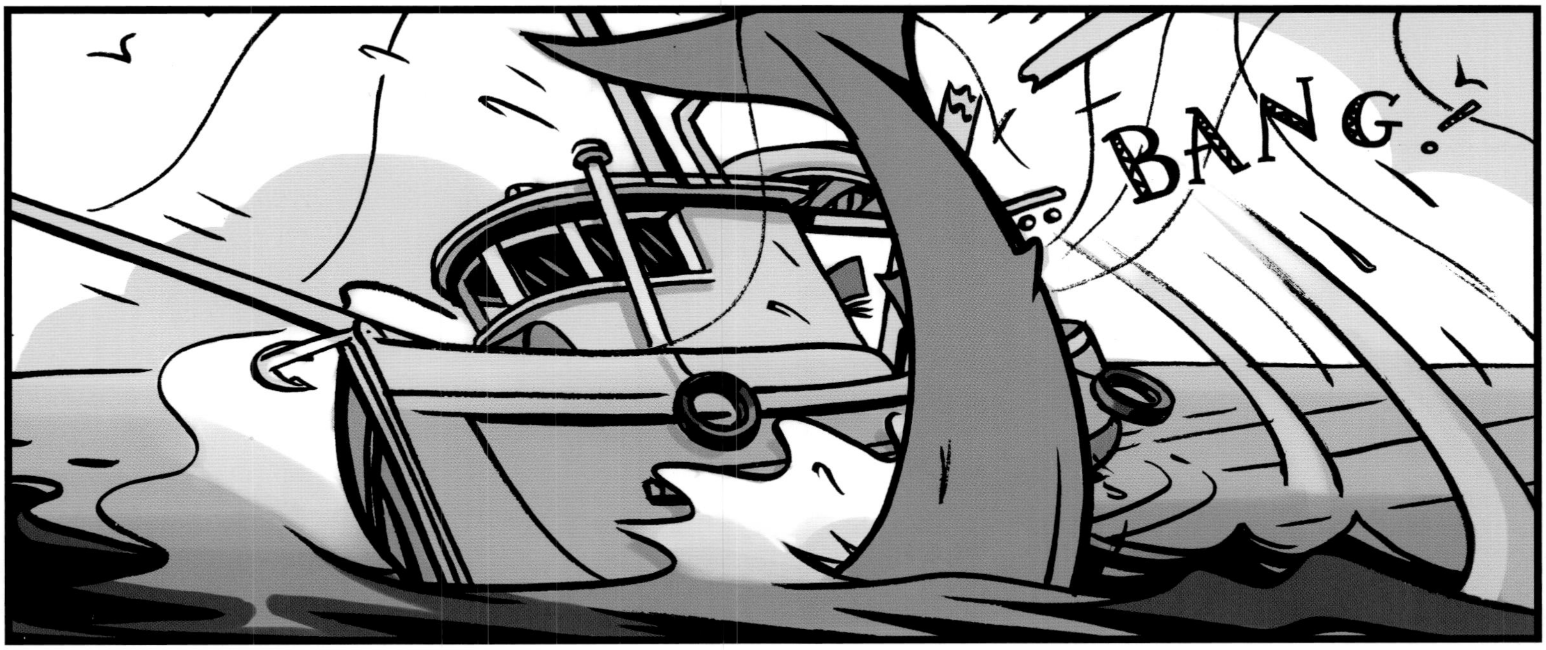
BANG!

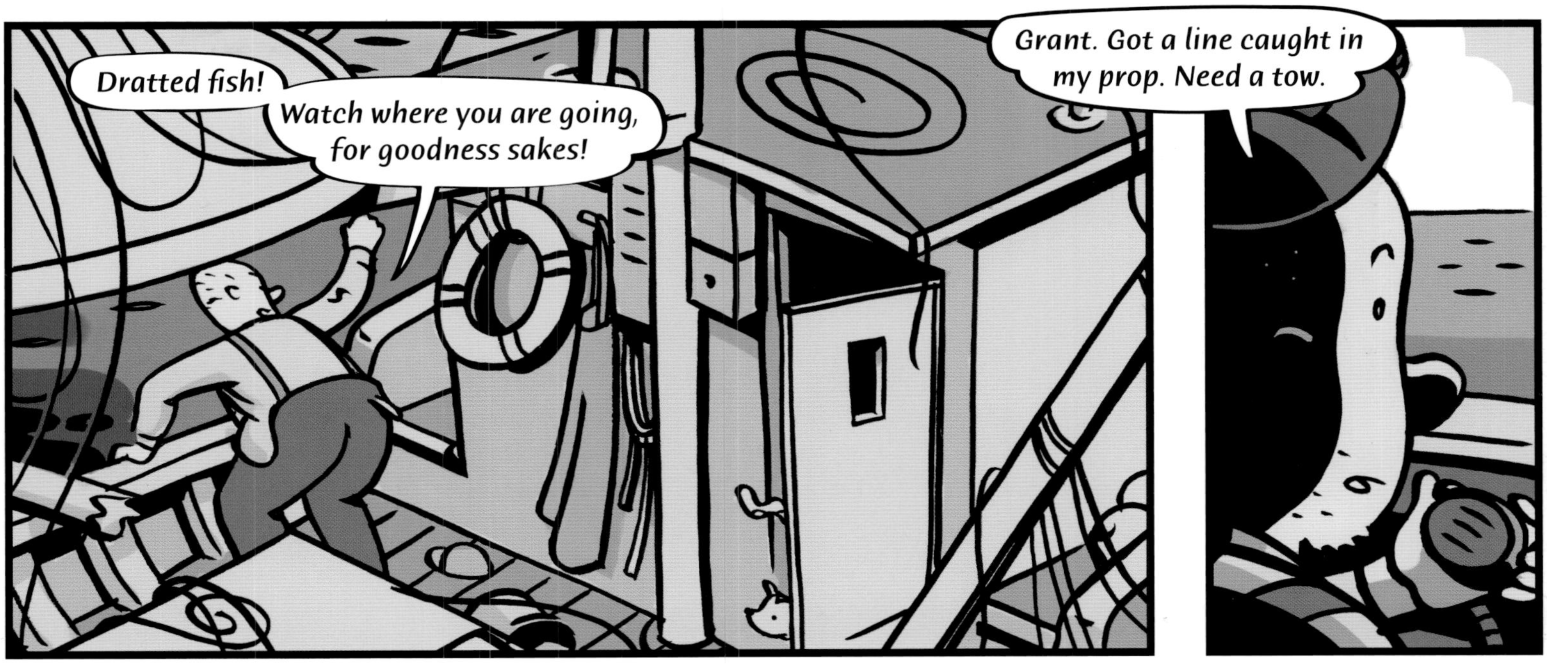
Dratted fish!
Watch where you are going, for goodness sakes!
Grant. Got a line caught in my prop. Need a tow.

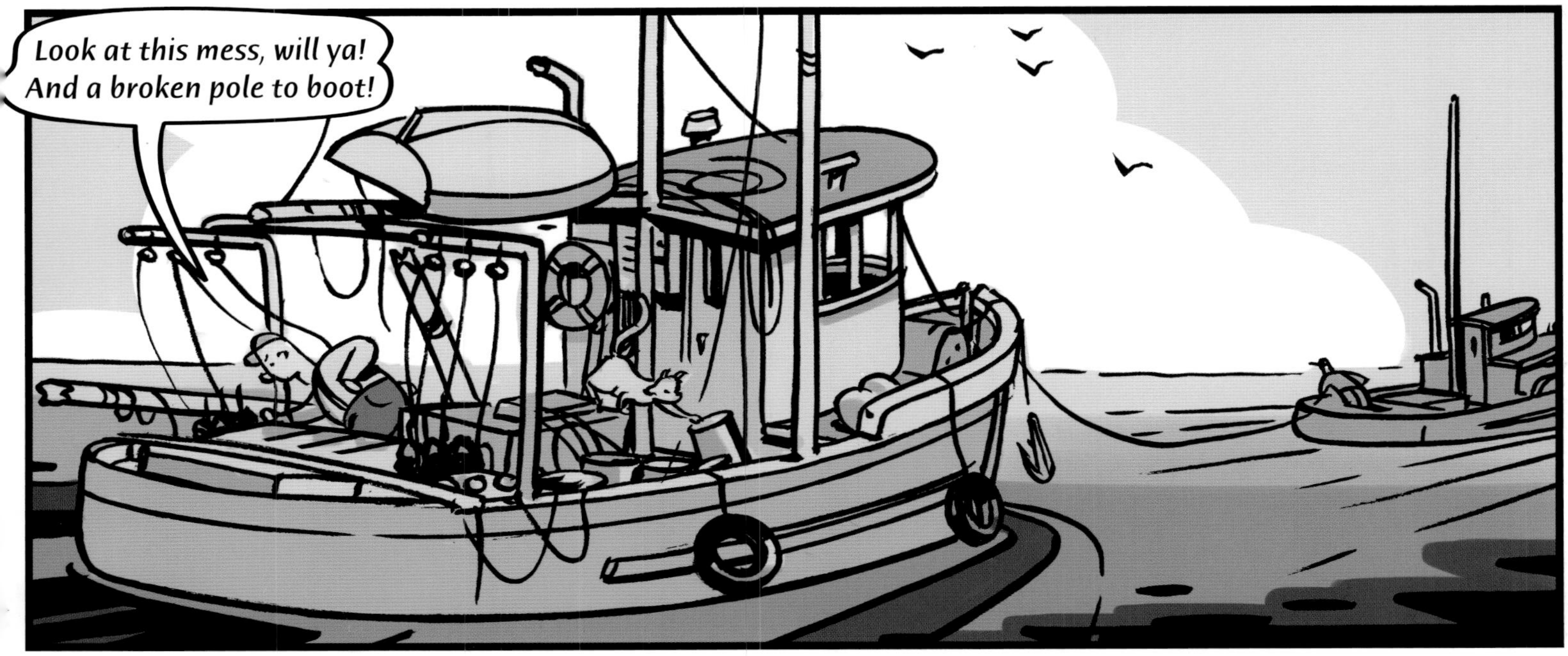
Look at this mess, will ya! And a broken pole to boot!

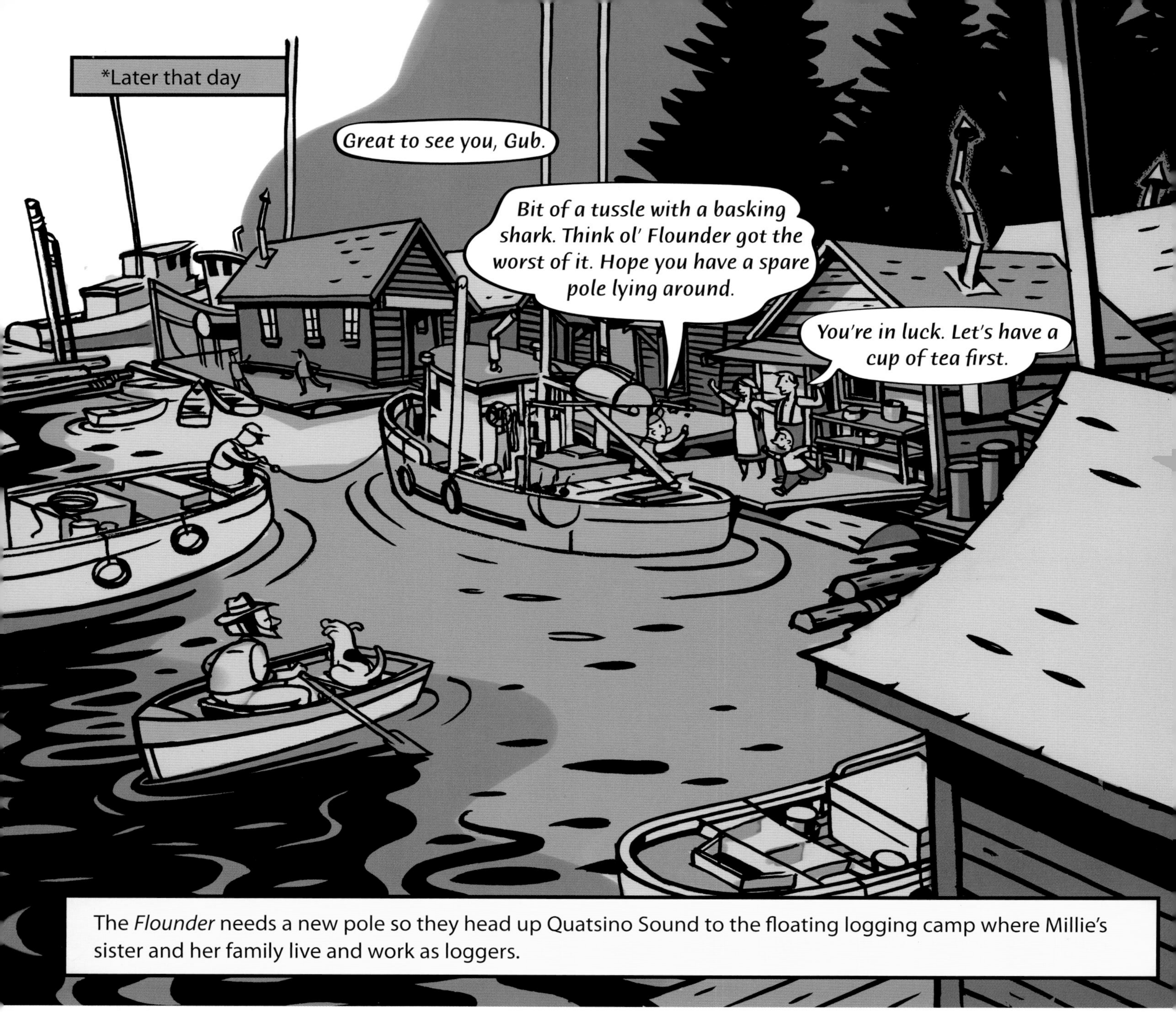
*Later that day
Great to see you, Gub.
Bit of a tussle with a basking shark. Think ol' Flounder got the worst of it. Hope you have a spare pole lying around.
You're in luck. Let's have a cup of tea first.
The *Flounder* needs a new pole so they head up Quatsino Sound to the floating logging camp where Millie's sister and her family live and work as loggers.

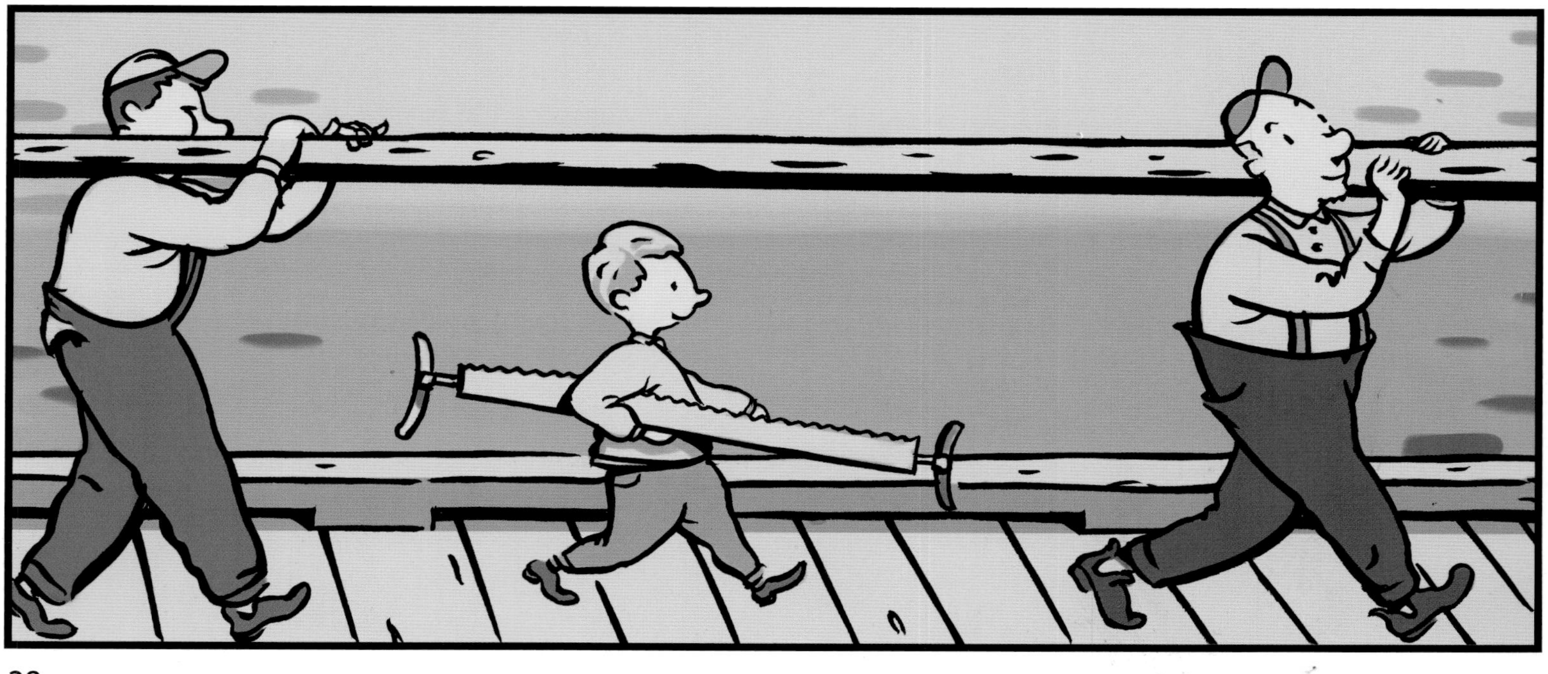

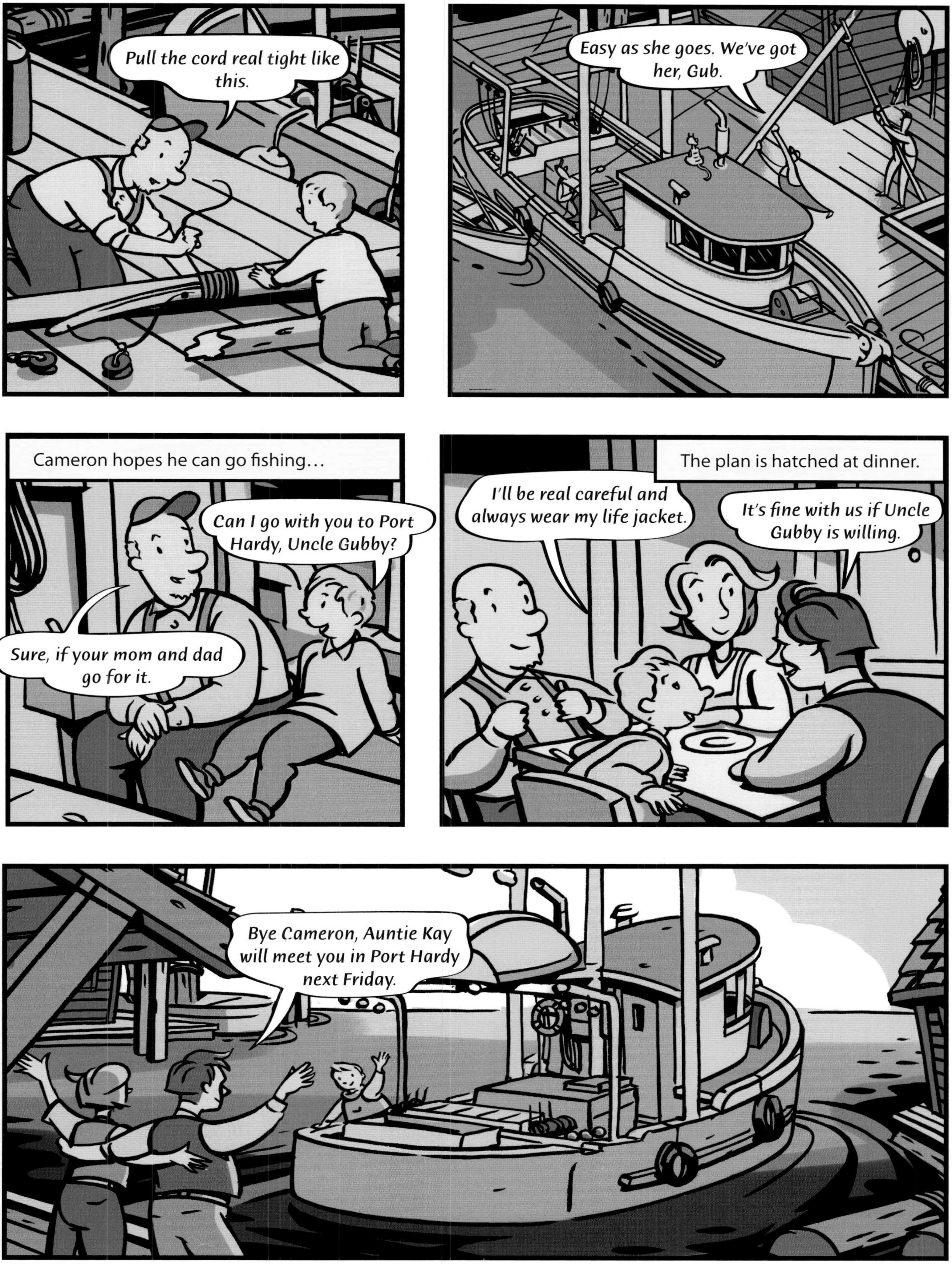

Pull the cord real tight like this.
Easy as she goes. We've got her, Gub.
Cameron hopes he can go fishing…
Can I go with you to Port Hardy, Uncle Gubby?
Sure, if your mom and dad go for it.
The plan is hatched at dinner.
I'll be real careful and always wear my life jacket.
It's fine with us if Uncle Gubby is willing.
Bye Cameron, Auntie Kay will meet you in Port Hardy next Friday.

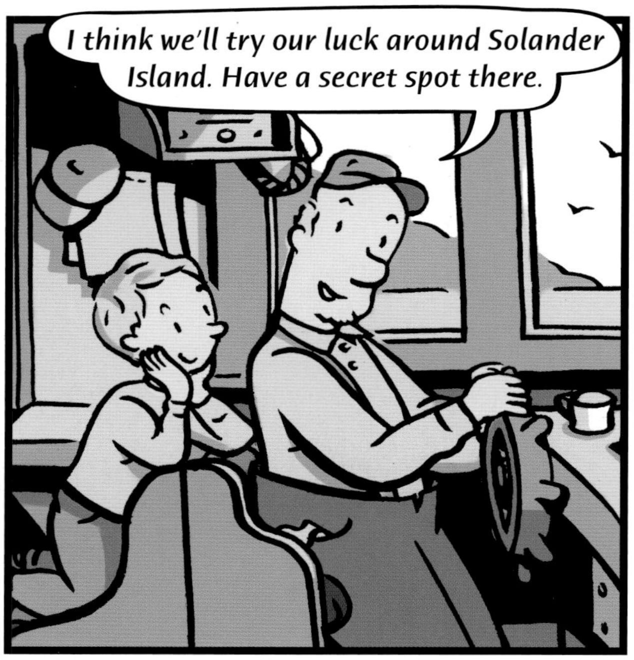
I think we'll try our luck around Solander Island. Have a secret spot there.

Cameron loves fishing but has always been too young to work the gear. Now that he is nine he hopes his uncle will let him do some real work. There are still some coho around so Gubby appreciates having an extra hand on board. And Puss will have a playmate.

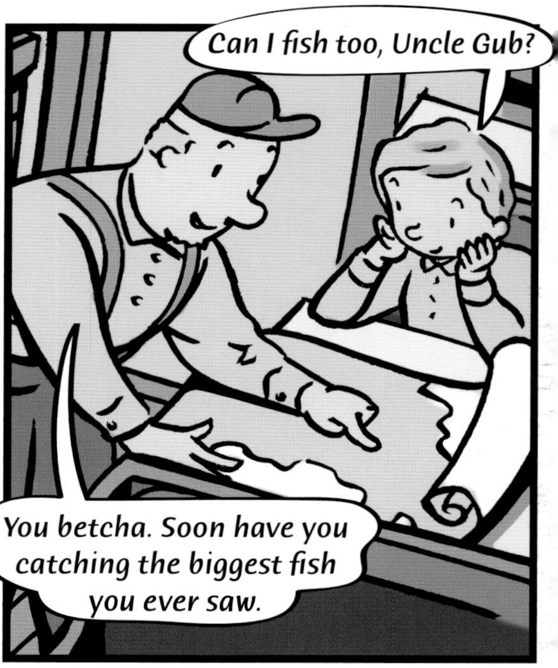
Can I fish too, Uncle Gub?
You betcha. Soon have you catching the biggest fish you ever saw.

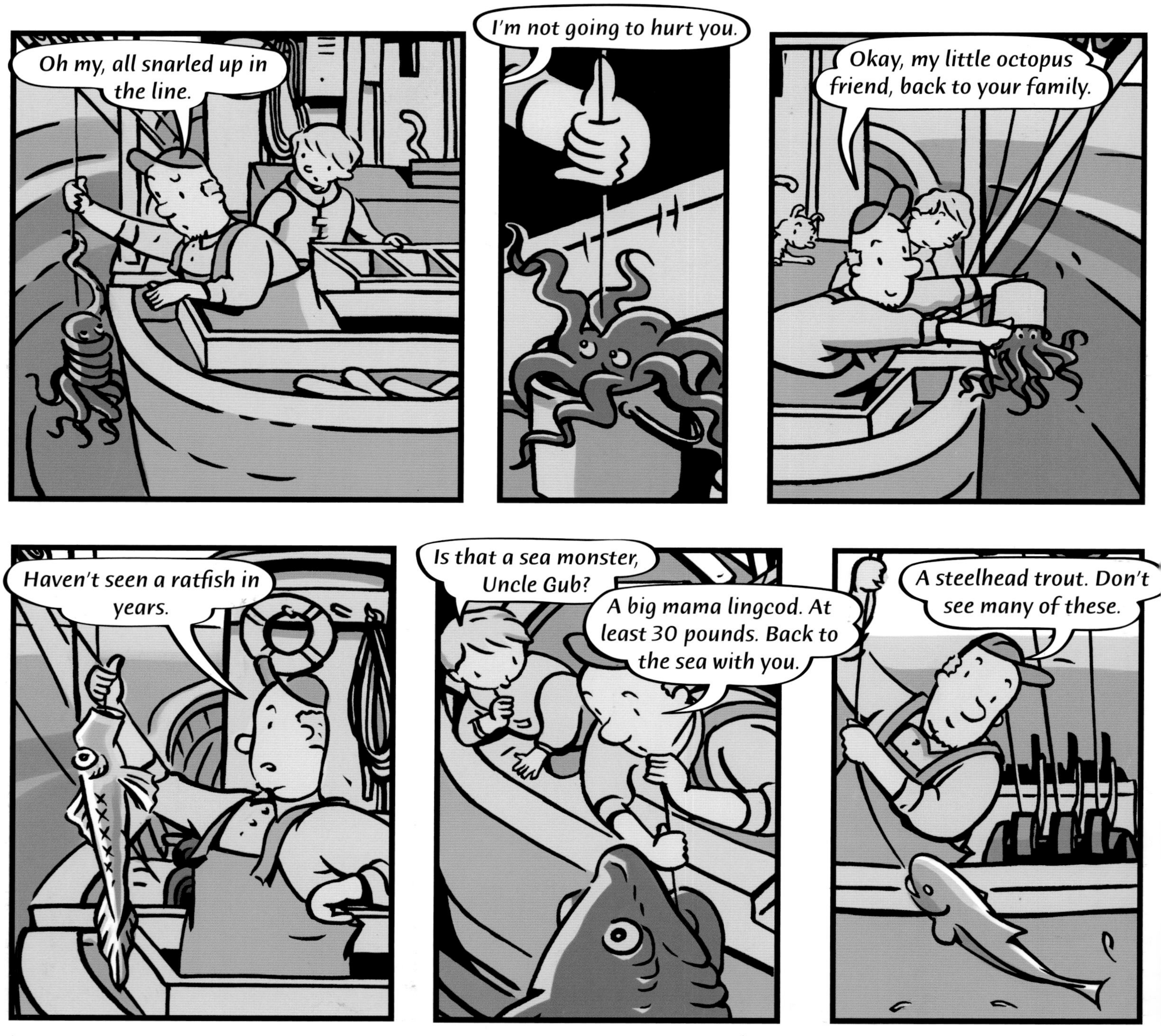
Oh my, all snarled up in the line.
I'm not going to hurt you.
Okay, my little octopus friend, back to your family.
Haven't seen a ratfish in years.
Is that a sea monster, Uncle Gub?
A big mama lingcod. At least 30 pounds. Back to the sea with you.
A steelhead trout. Don't see many of these.

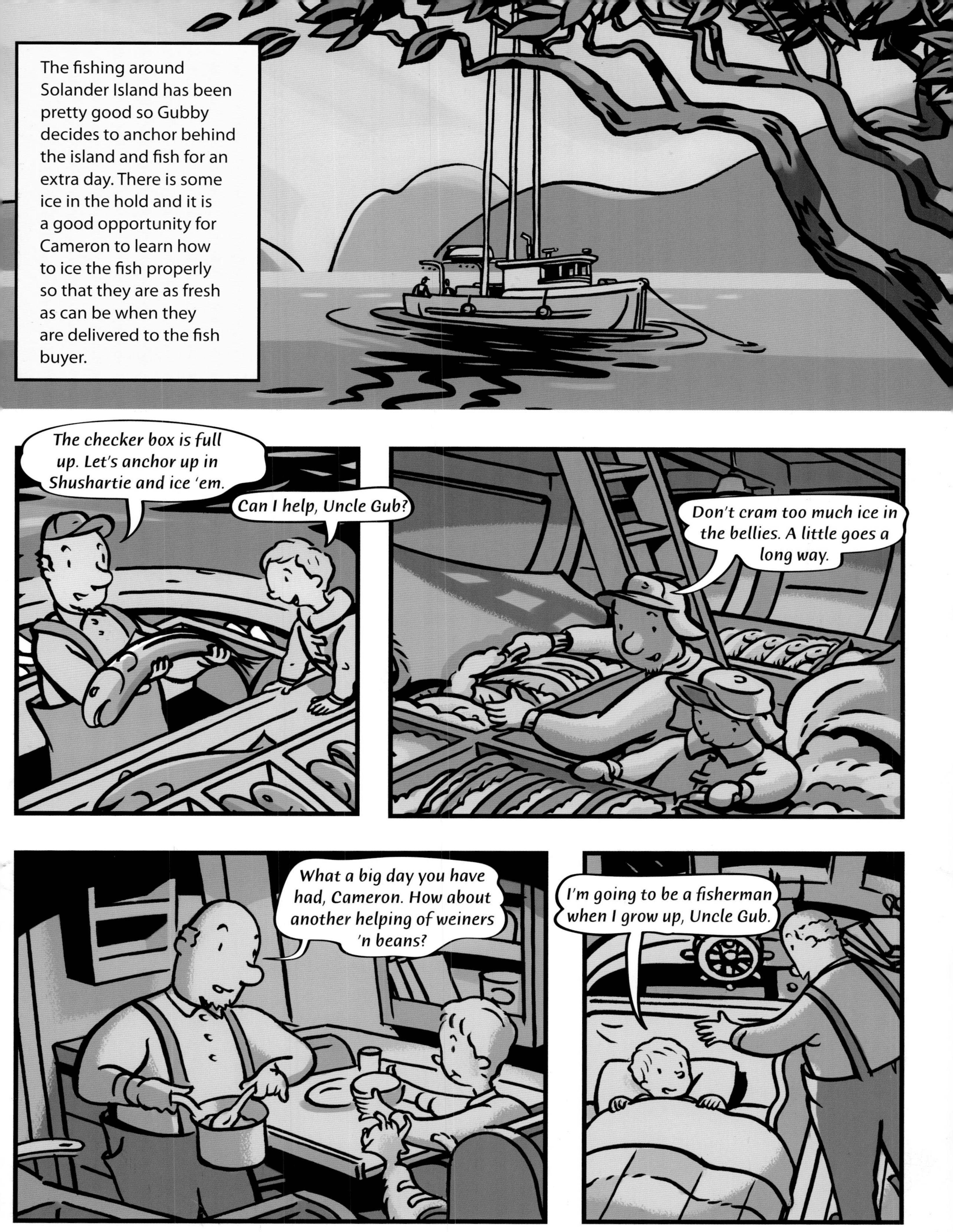
The fishing around Solander Island has been pretty good so Gubby decides to anchor behind the island and fish for an extra day. There is some ice in the hold and it is a good opportunity for Cameron to learn how to ice the fish properly so that they are as fresh as can be when they are delivered to the fish buyer.
The checker box is full up. Let's anchor up in Shushartie and ice 'em.
Can I help, Uncle Gub?
Don't cram too much ice in the bellies. A little goes a long way.
What a big day you have had, Cameron. How about another helping of weiners 'n beans?
I'm going to be a fisherman when I grow up, Uncle Gub.

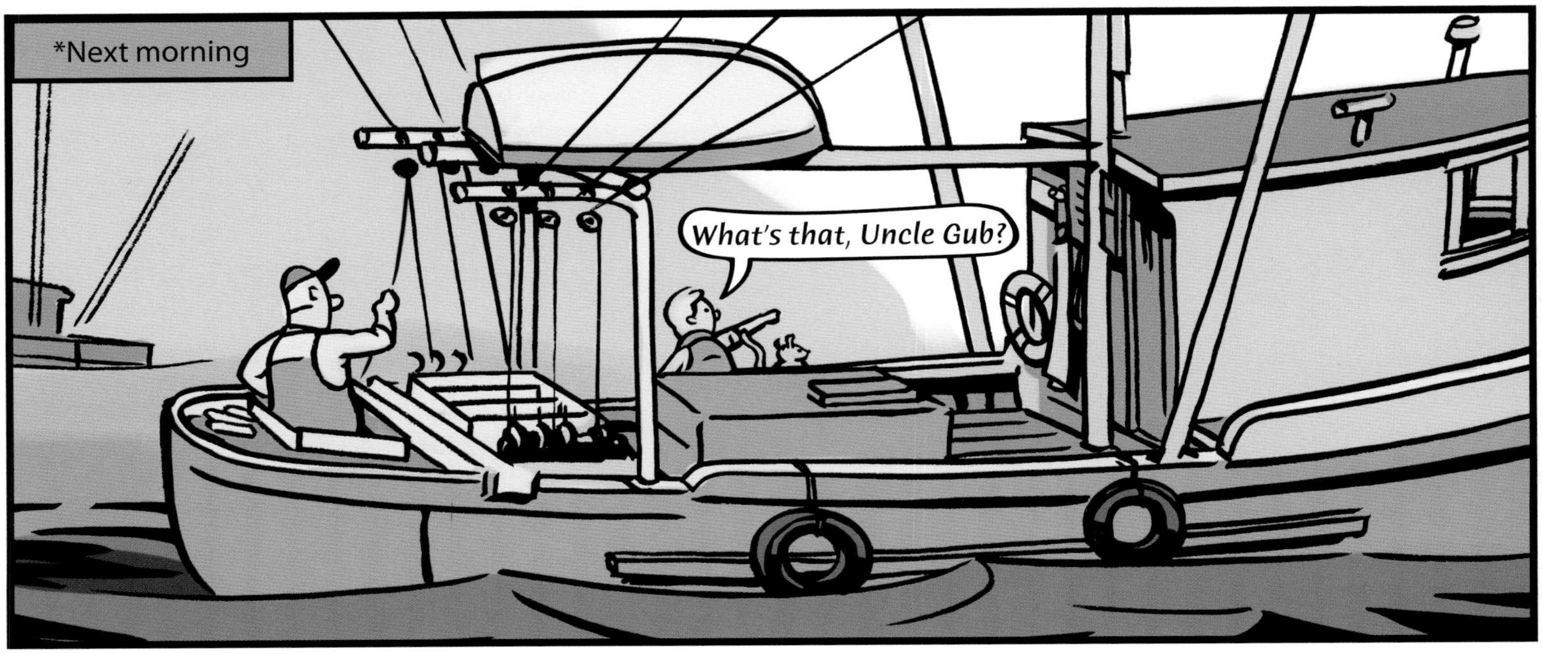
*Next morning
What's that, Uncle Gub?

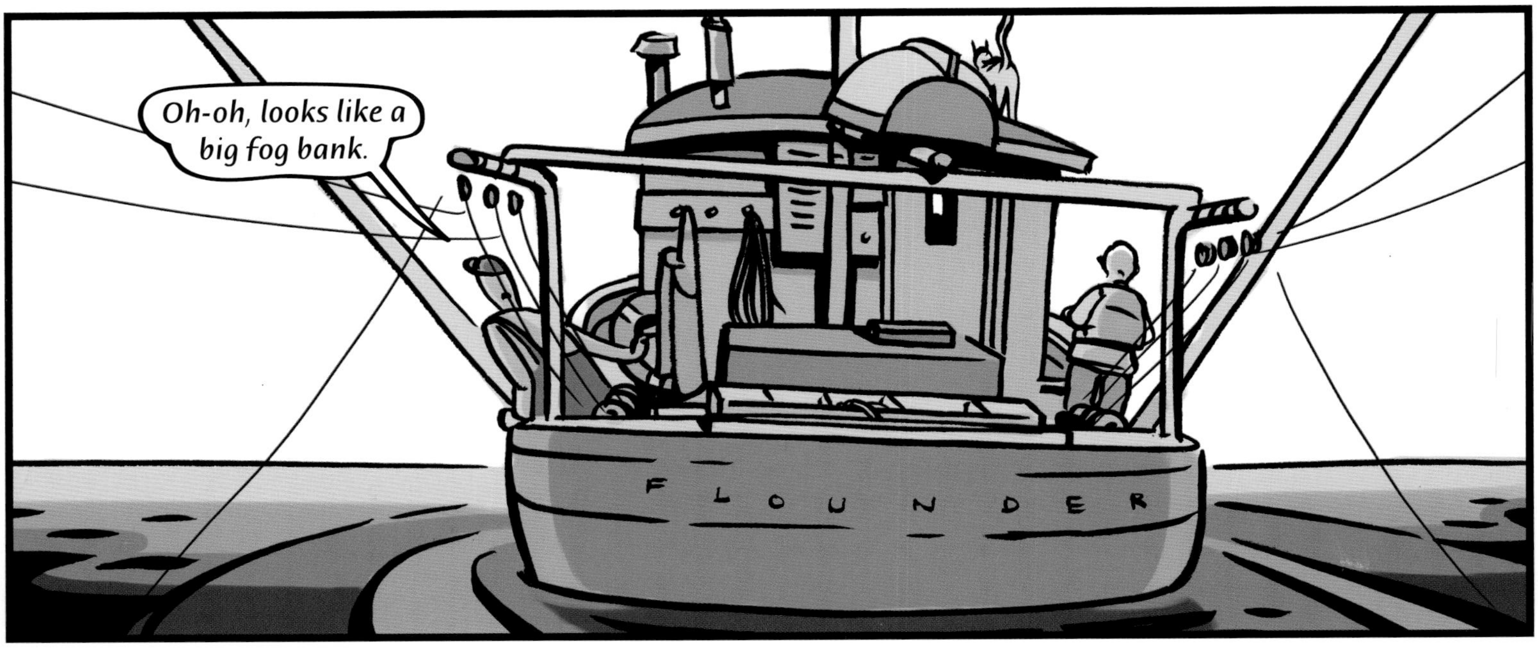
Oh-oh, looks like a big fog bank.
FLOUNDER

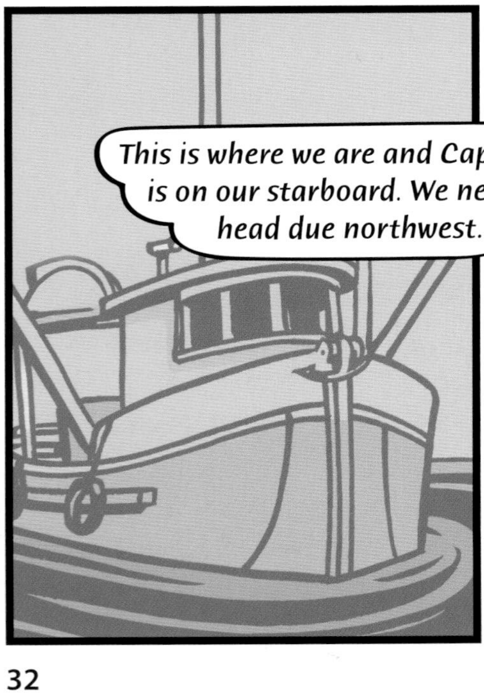
This is where we are and Cape Cook is on our starboard. We need to head due northwest.

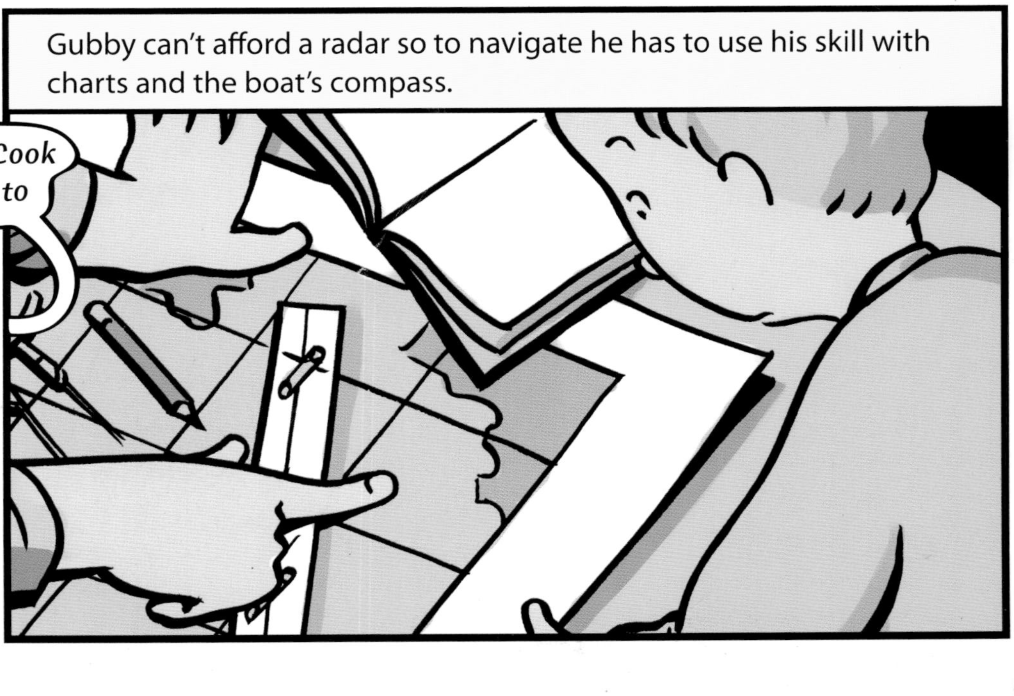
Gubby can't afford a radar so to navigate he has to use his skill with charts and the boat's compass.

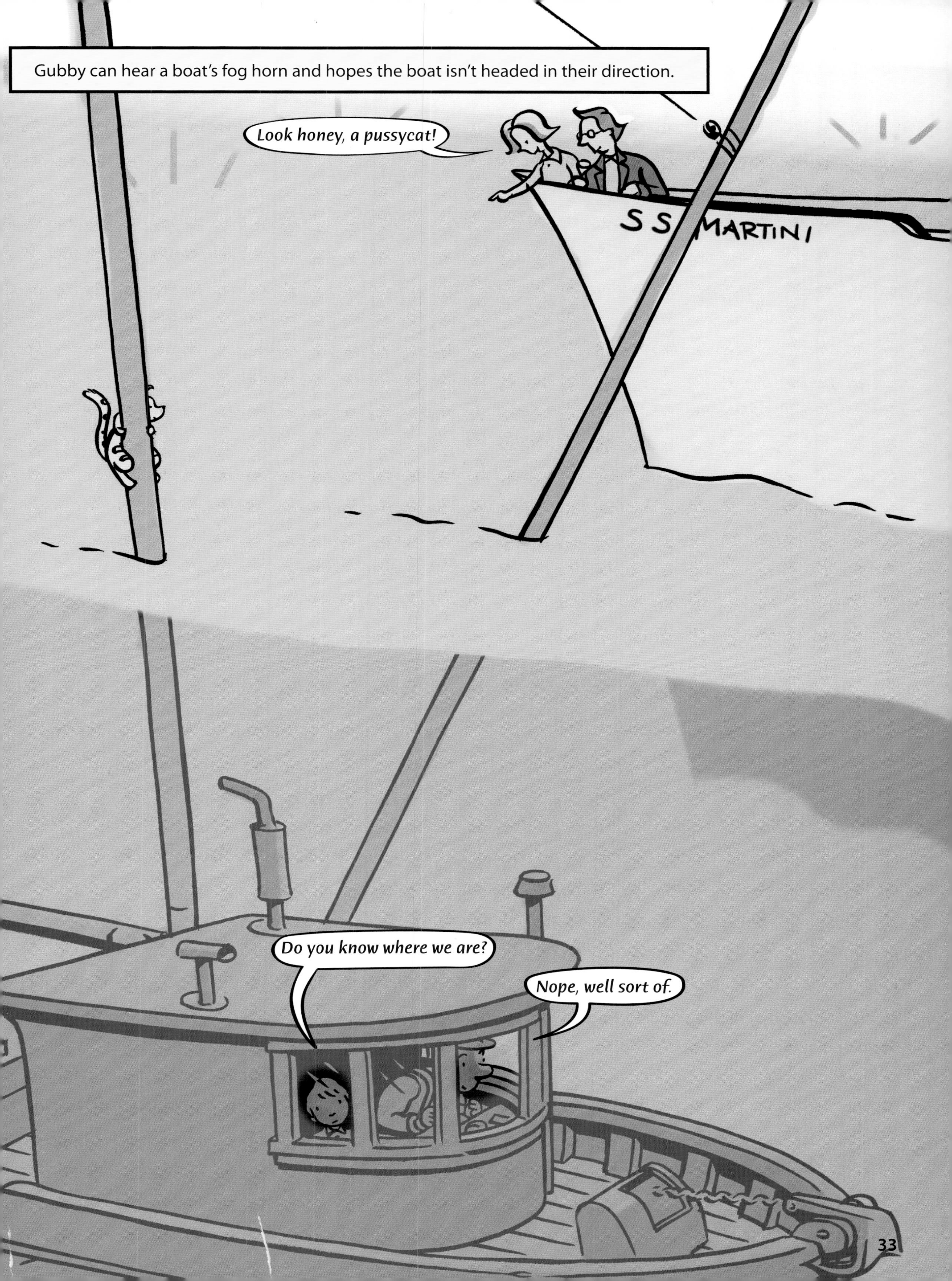
Gubby can hear a boat's fog horn and hopes the boat isn't headed in their direction.
Look honey, a pussycat!
SS MARTINI
Do you know where we are?
Nope, well sort of.

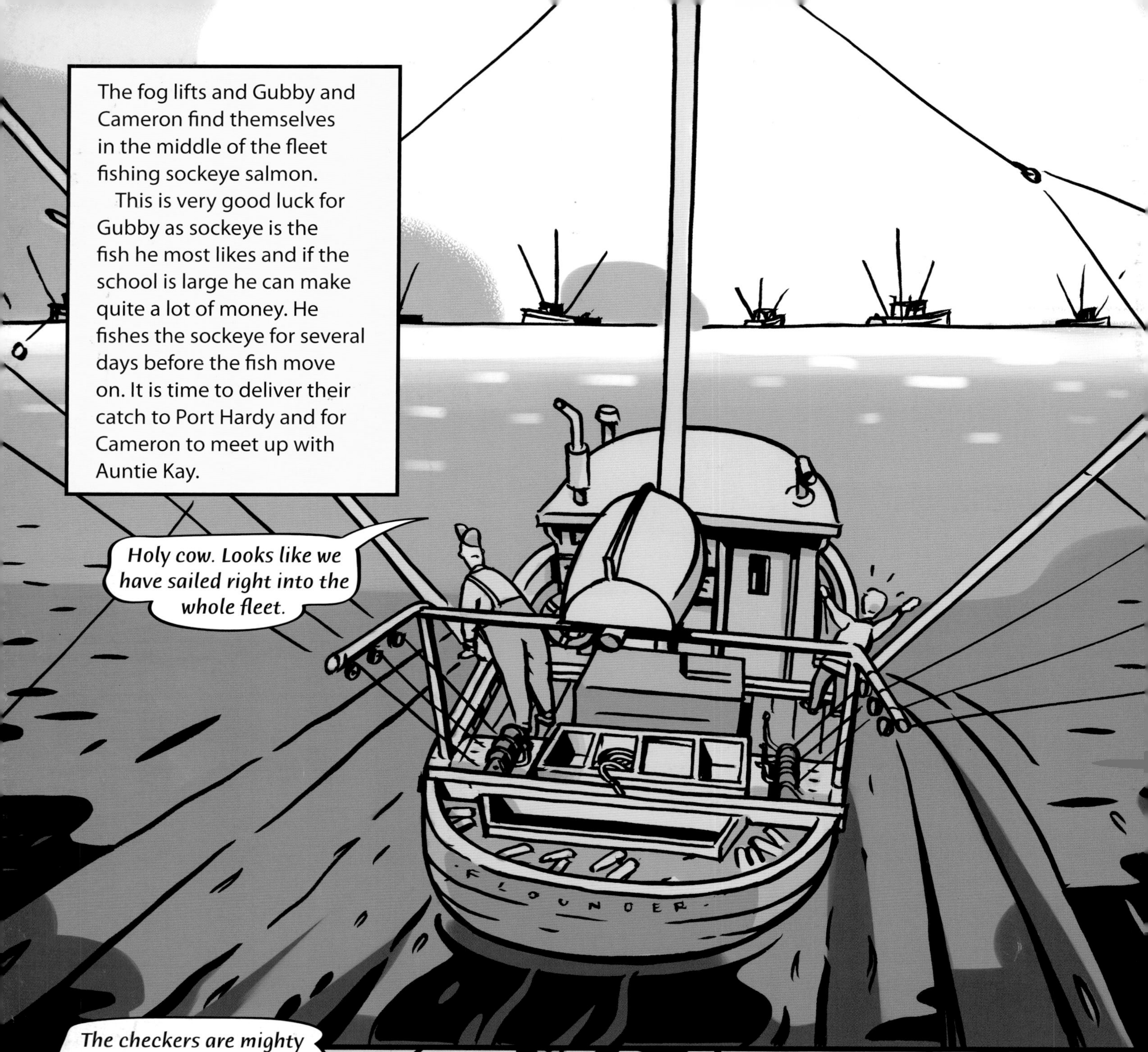
The fog lifts and Gubby and Cameron find themselves in the middle of the fleet fishing sockeye salmon.
This is very good luck for Gubby as sockeye is the fish he most likes and if the school is large he can make quite a lot of money. He fishes the sockeye for several days before the fish move on. It is time to deliver their catch to Port Hardy and for Cameron to meet up with Auntie Kay.
Holy cow. Looks like we have sailed right into the whole fleet.
FLOUNDER

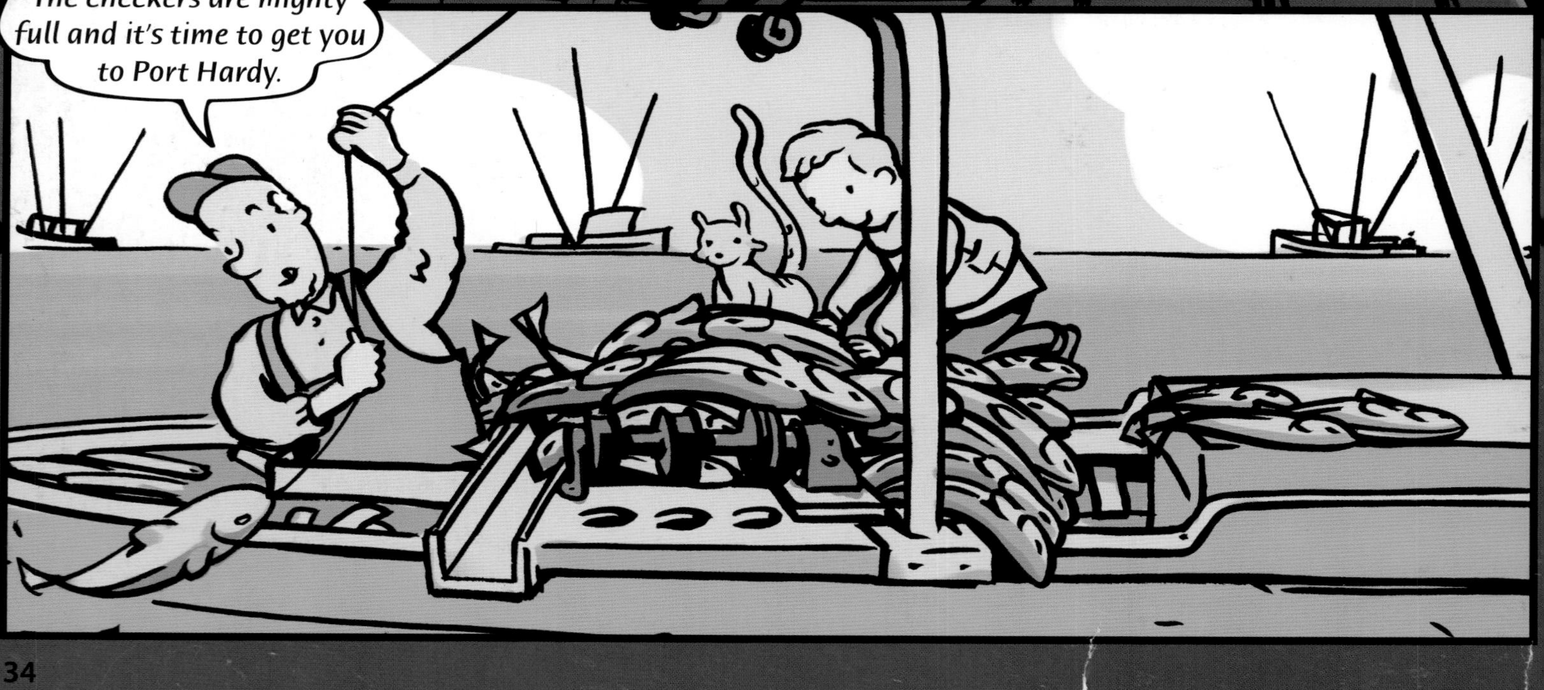
The checkers are mighty full and it's time to get you to Port Hardy.

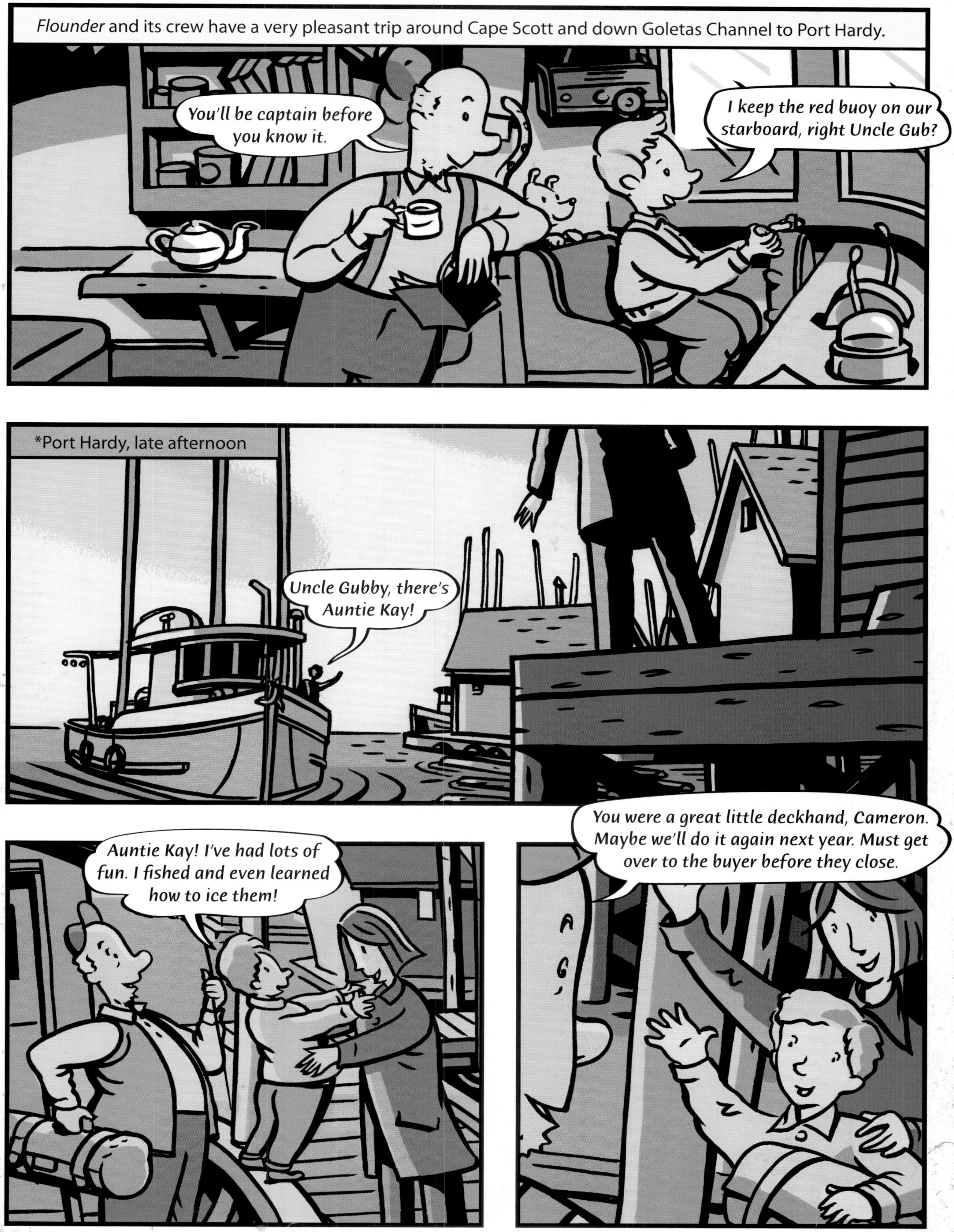
Flounder and its crew have a very pleasant trip around Cape Scott and down Goletas Channel to Port Hardy.
You'll be captain before you know it.
I keep the red buoy on our starboard, right Uncle Gub?
*Port Hardy, late afternoon
Uncle Gubby, there's Auntie Kay!
Auntie Kay! I've had lots of fun. I fished and even learned how to ice them!
You were a great little deckhand, Cameron. Maybe we'll do it again next year. Must get over to the buyer before they close.

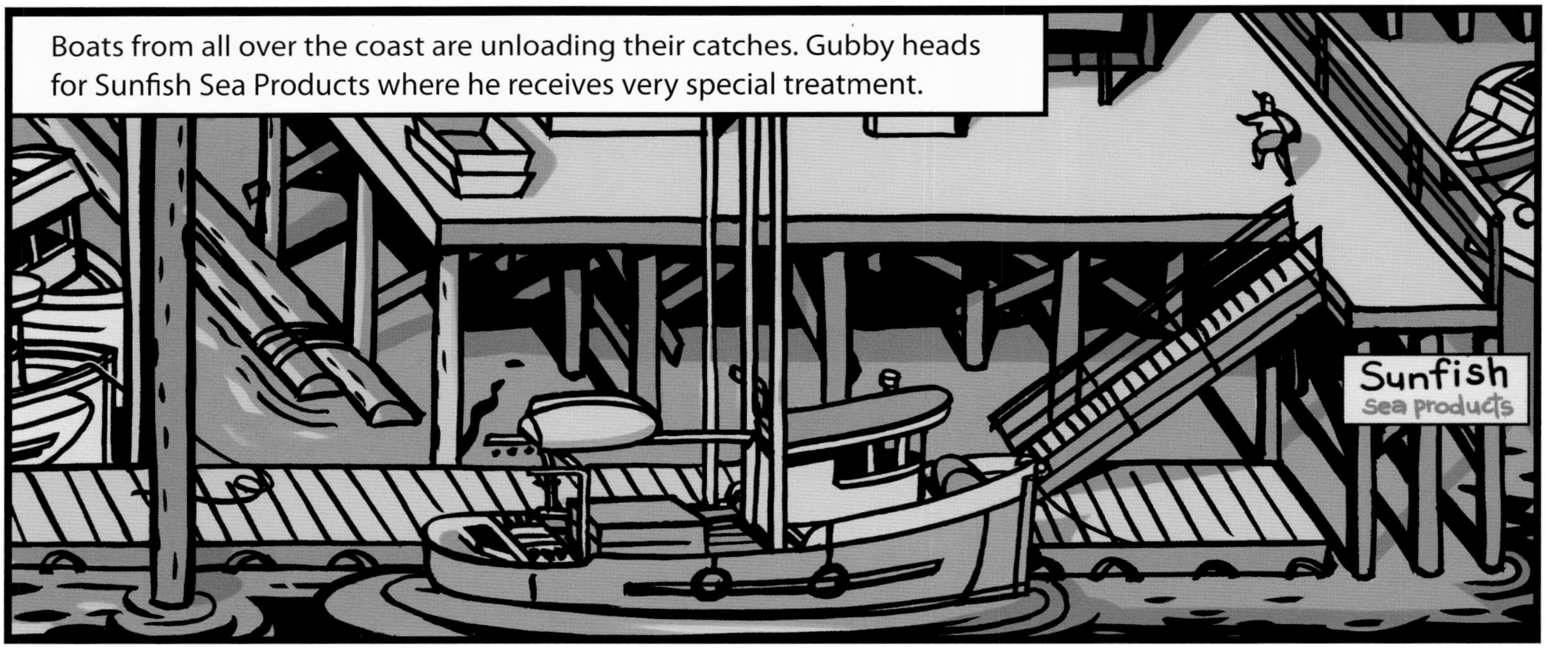
Boats from all over the coast are unloading their catches. Gubby heads for Sunfish Sea Products where he receives very special treatment.
Sunfish
sea products

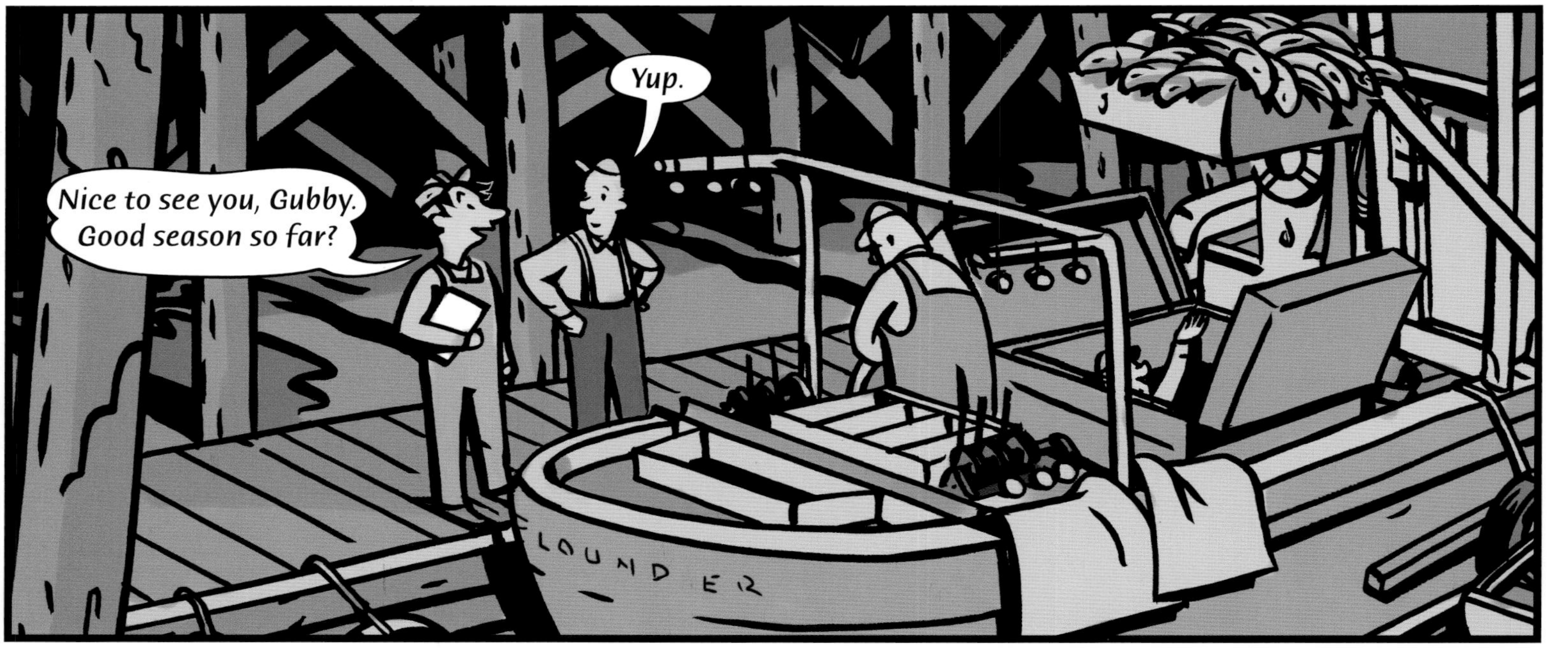
Nice to see you, Gubby. Good season so far?
Yup.
LOUNDER

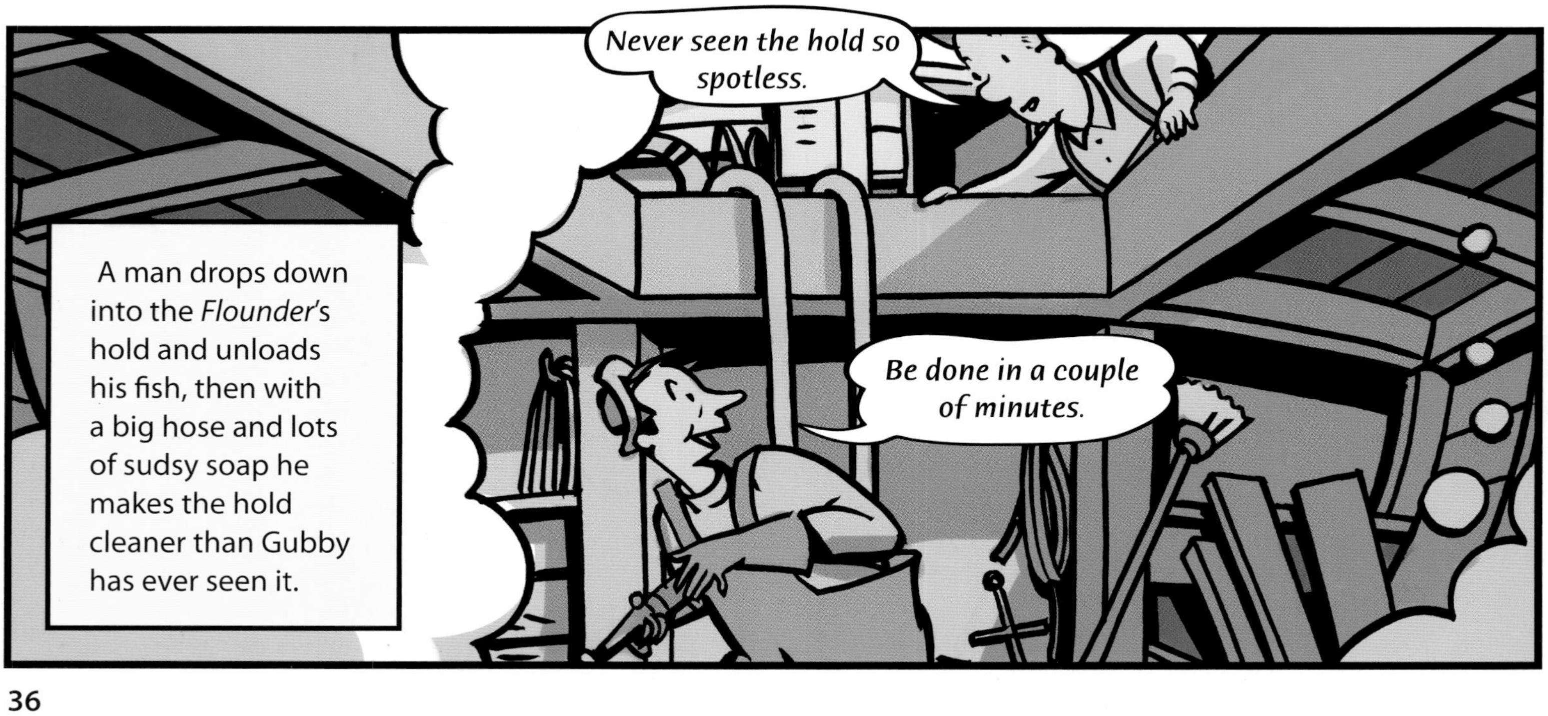
Never seen the hold so spotless.
A man drops down into the *Flounder*'s hold and unloads his fish, then with a big hose and lots of sudsy soap he makes the hold cleaner than Gubby has ever seen it.
Be done in a couple of minutes.

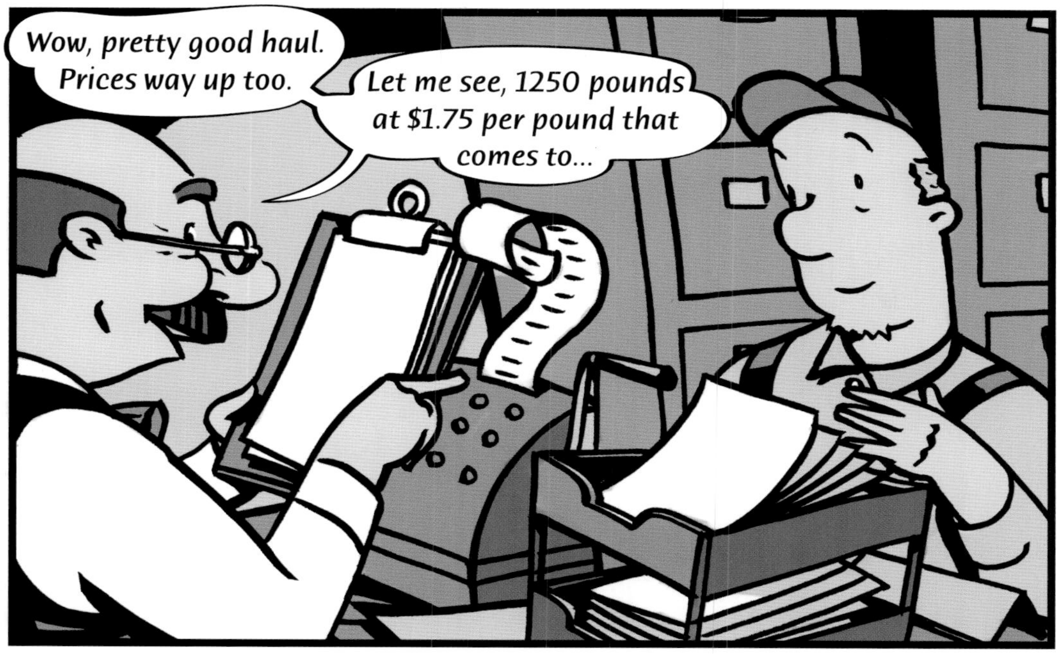
Wow, pretty good haul. Prices way up too.
Let me see, 1250 pounds at $1.75 per pound that comes to...

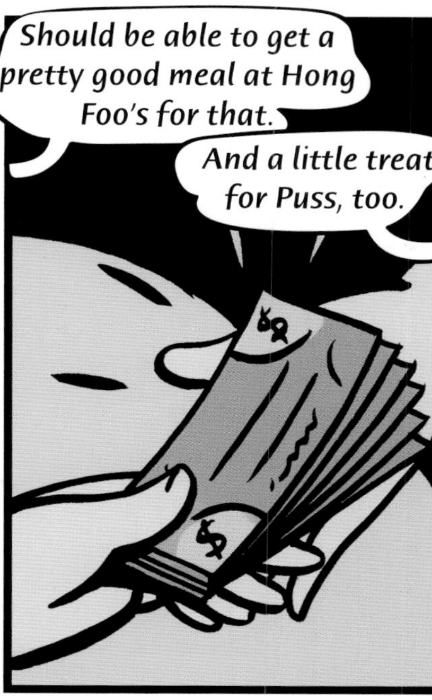
Should be able to get a pretty good meal at Hong Foo's for that.
And a little treat for Puss, too.

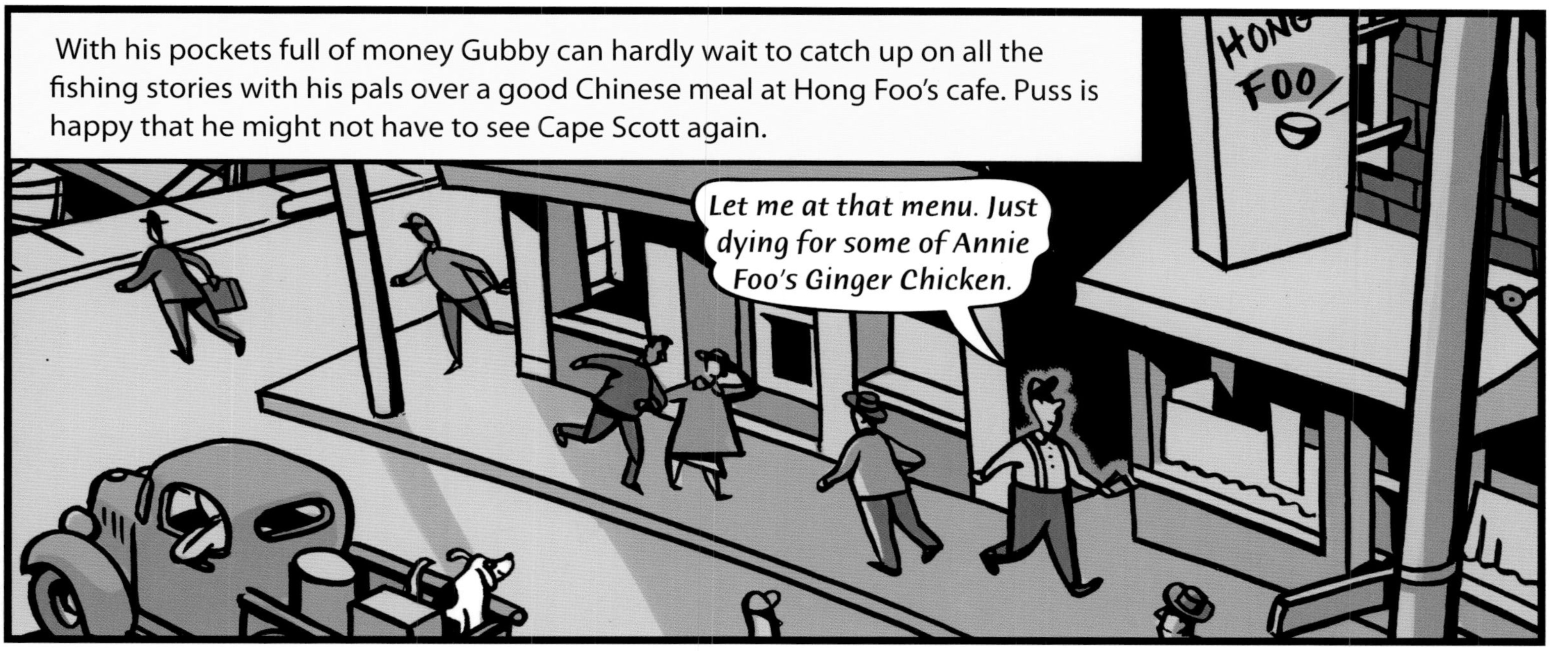
With his pockets full of money Gubby can hardly wait to catch up on all the fishing stories with his pals over a good Chinese meal at Hong Foo's cafe. Puss is happy that he might not have to see Cape Scott again.
HONG FOO
Let me at that menu. Just dying for some of Annie Foo's Ginger Chicken.

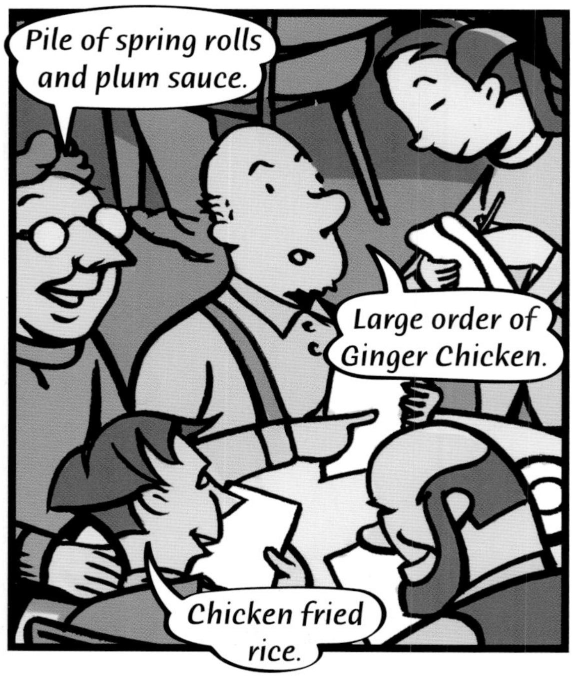
Pile of spring rolls and plum sauce.
Large order of Ginger Chicken.
Chicken fried rice.

With the fishing season coming to an end and salmon all along the coast heading for their river spawning grounds, Gubby and his pals discuss where they'll fish next.

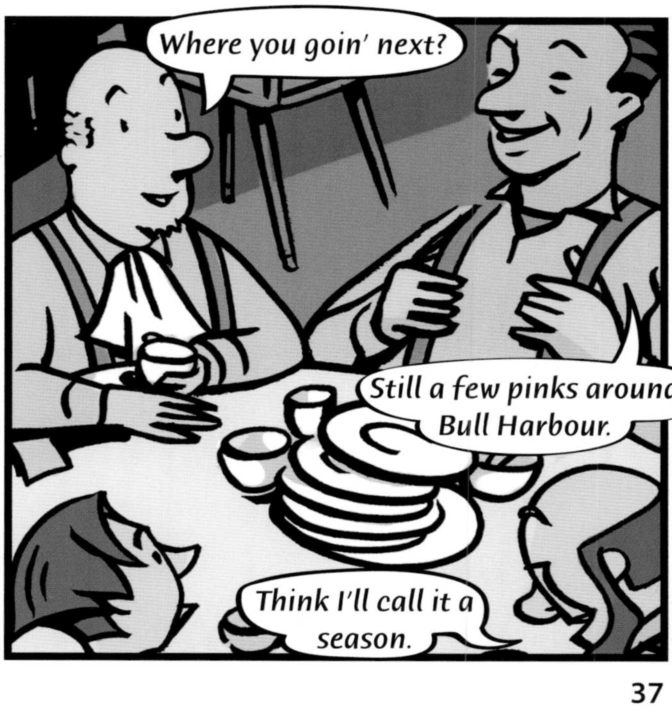
Where you goin' next?
Still a few pinks around Bull Harbour.
Think I'll call it a season.

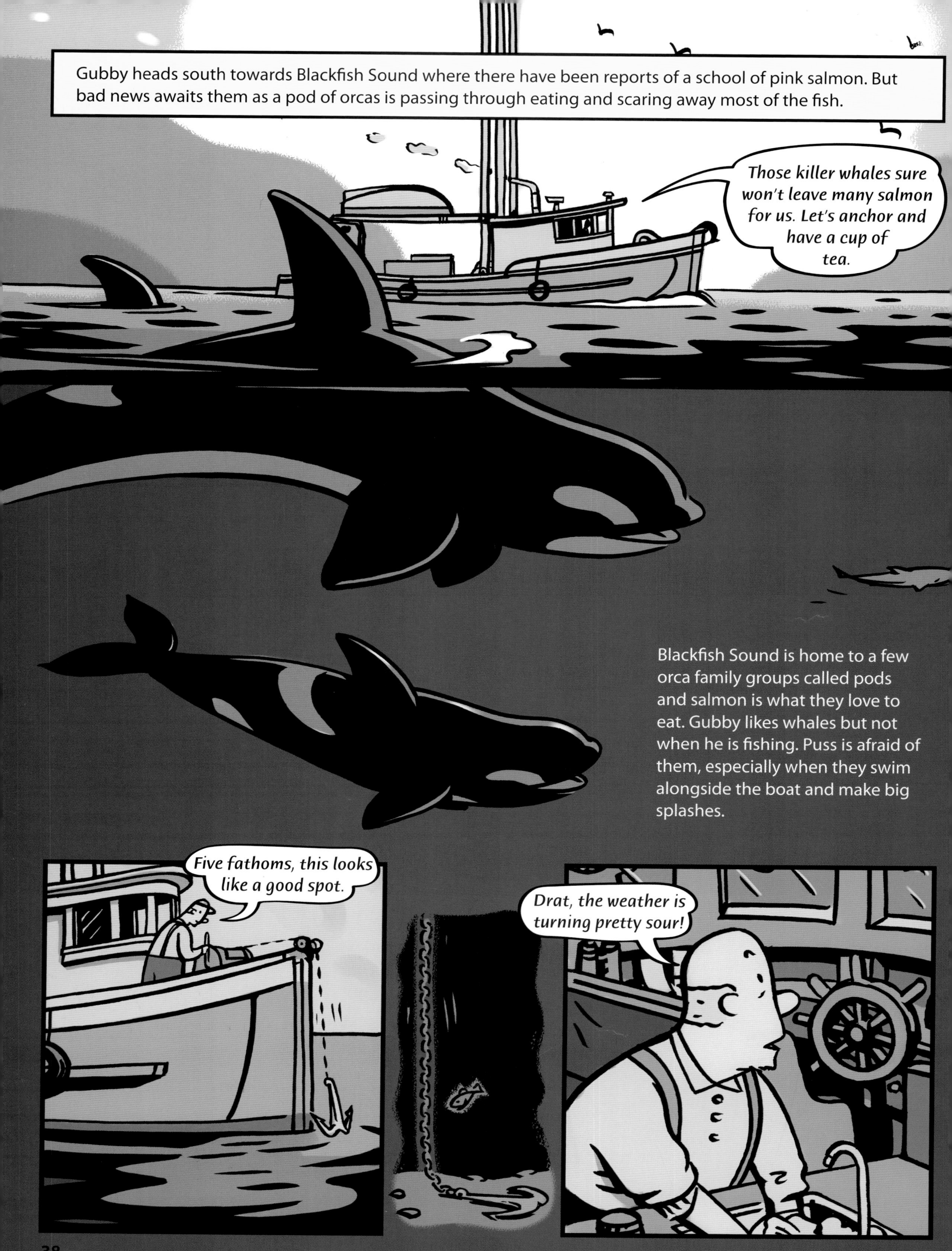
Gubby heads south towards Blackfish Sound where there have been reports of a school of pink salmon. But bad news awaits them as a pod of orcas is passing through eating and scaring away most of the fish.
Those killer whales sure won't leave many salmon for us. Let's anchor and have a cup of tea.
Blackfish Sound is home to a few orca family groups called pods and salmon is what they love to eat. Gubby likes whales but not when he is fishing. Puss is afraid of them, especially when they swim alongside the boat and make big splashes.
Five fathoms, this looks like a good spot.
Drat, the weather is turning pretty sour!

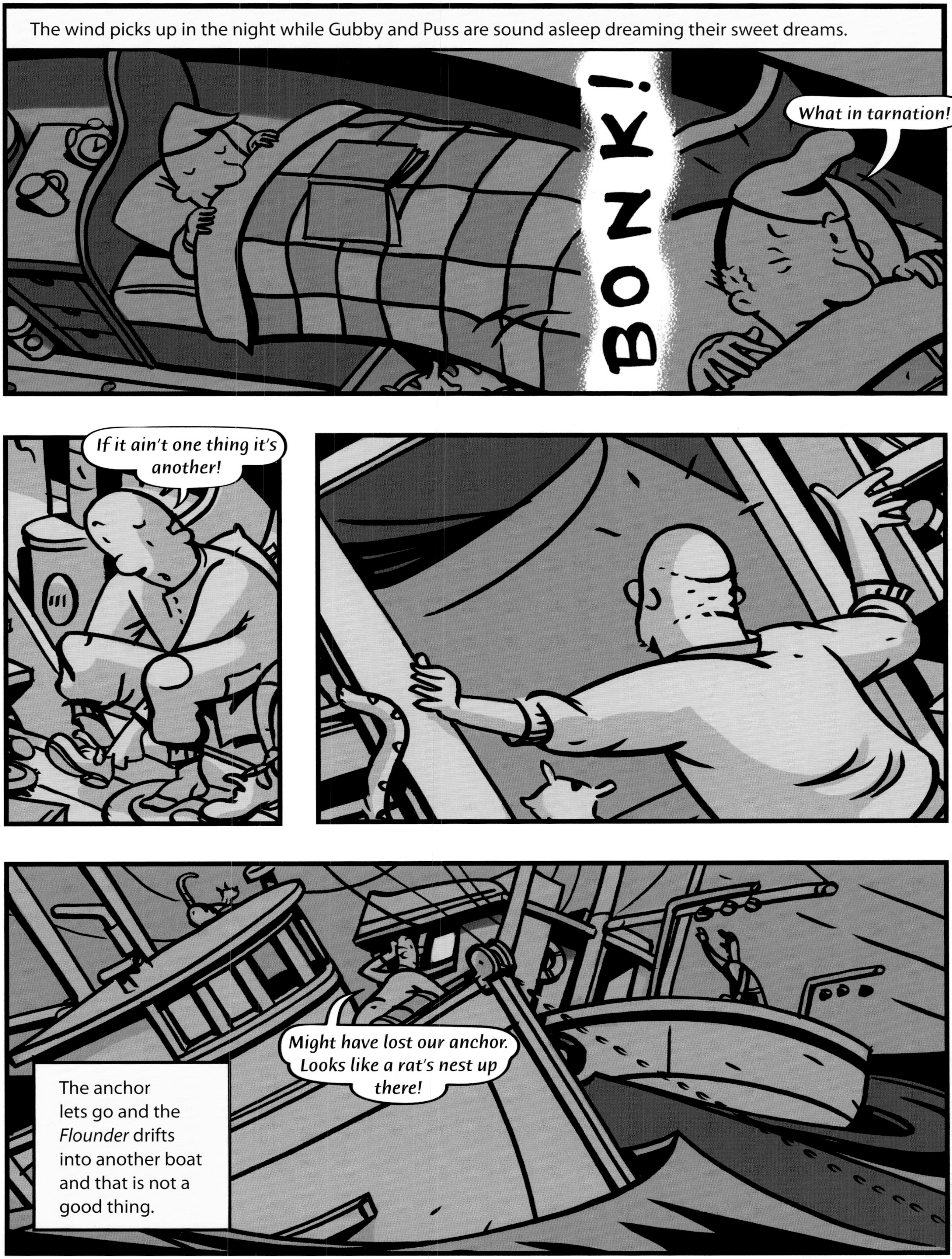
The wind picks up in the night while Gubby and Puss are sound asleep dreaming their sweet dreams.
BONK!
What in tarnation!!
If it ain't one thing it's another!
The anchor lets go and the *Flounder* drifts into another boat and that is not a good thing.
Might have lost our anchor. Looks like a rat's nest up there!

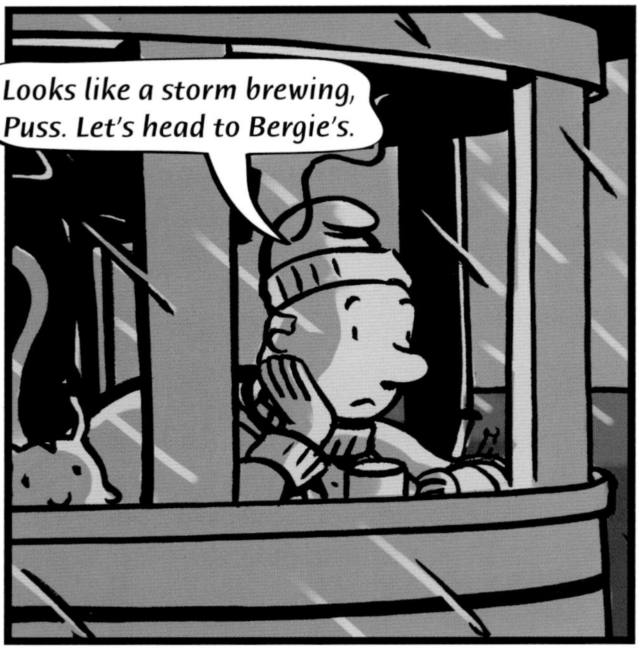
Looks like a storm brewing, Puss. Let's head to Bergie's.

Crashing into another boat is the final straw for Gubby. It is time to head south and have a little visit with cousin Bergie in Beaver Inlet. They hope she'll be home and not on one of her hunting trips.

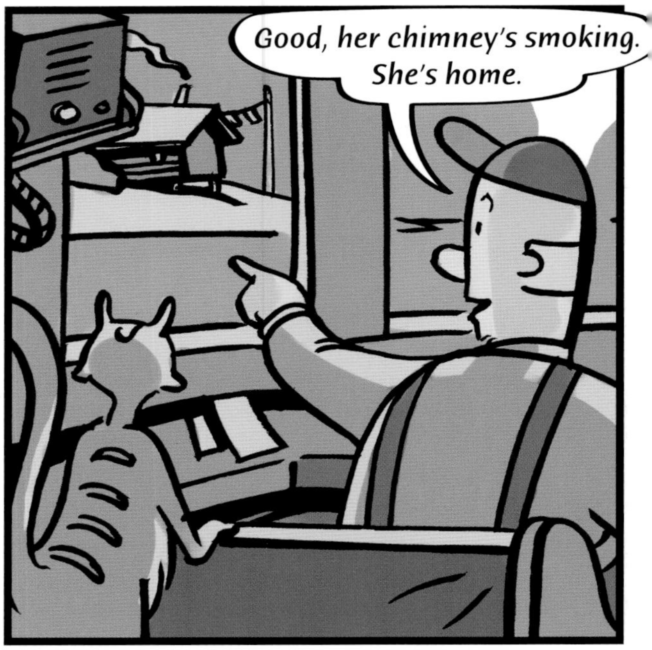
Good, her chimney's smoking. She's home.

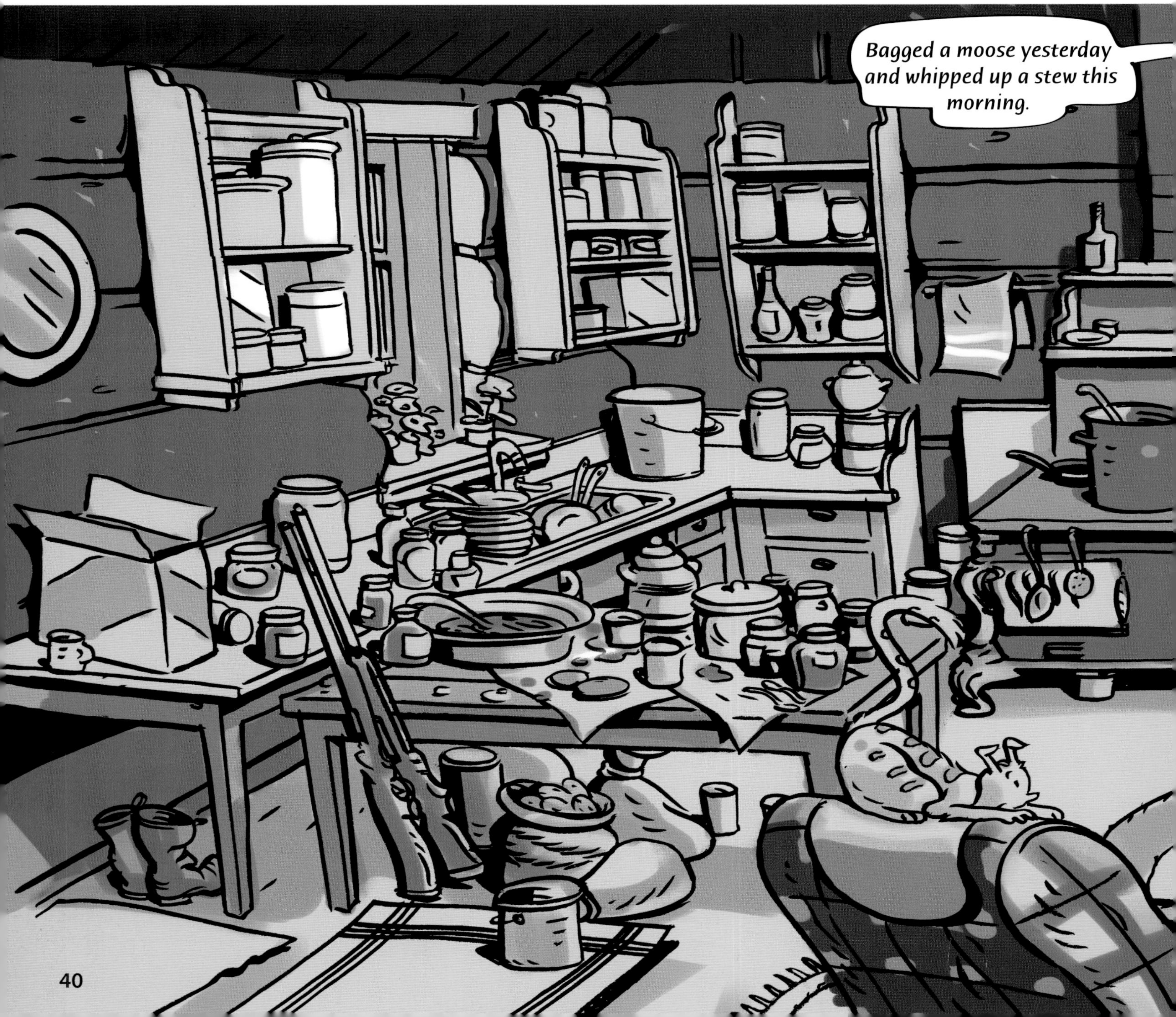
Bagged a moose yesterday and whipped up a stew this morning.

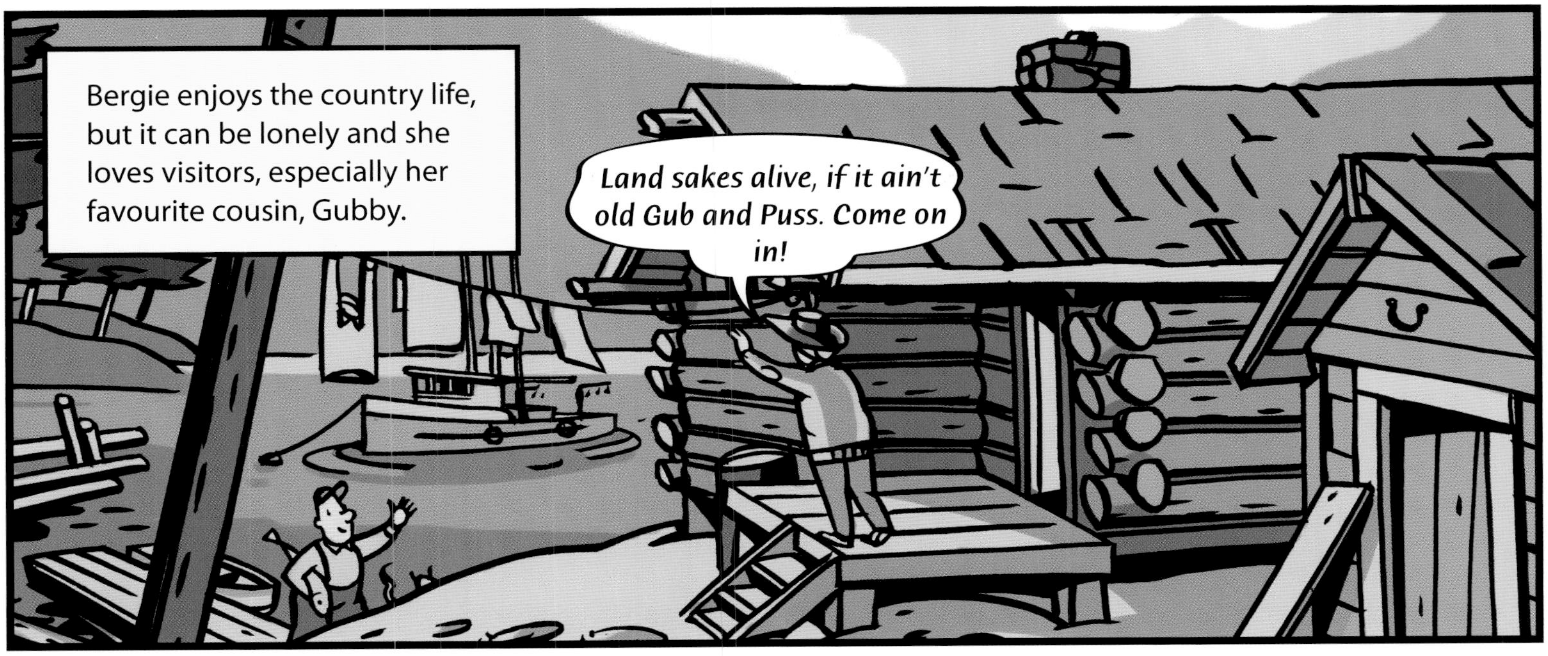
Bergie enjoys the country life, but it can be lonely and she loves visitors, especially her favourite cousin, Gubby.
Land sakes alive, if it ain't old Gub and Puss. Come on in!

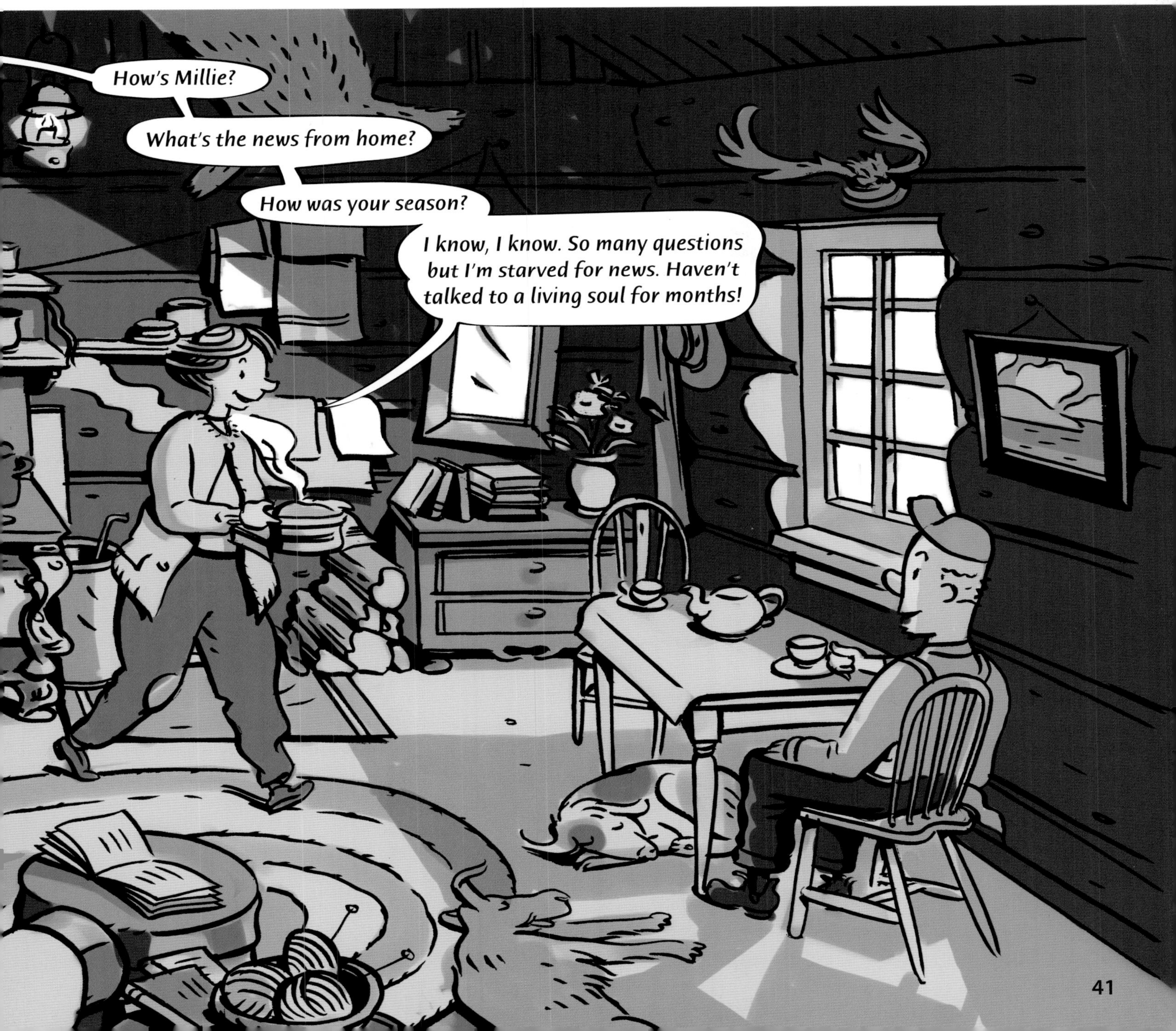
How's Millie?
What's the news from home?
How was your season?
I know, I know. So many questions but I'm starved for news. Haven't talked to a living soul for months!

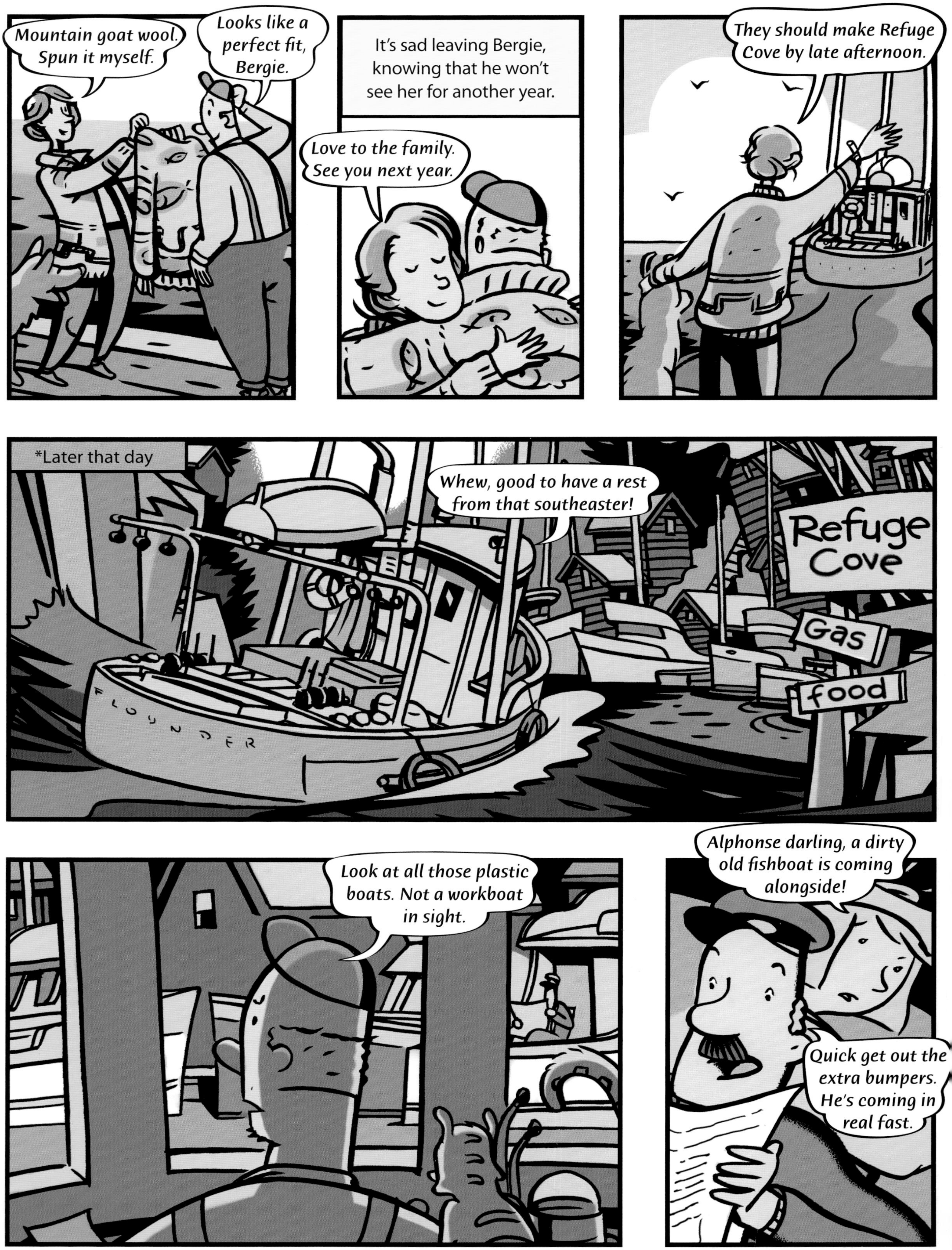
Mountain goat wool. Spun it myself.
Looks like a perfect fit, Bergie.
It's sad leaving Bergie, knowing that he won't see her for another year.
Love to the family. See you next year.
They should make Refuge Cove by late afternoon.
*Later that day
Whew, good to have a rest from that southeaster!
Refuge Cove
Gas
food
FLOUNDER
Look at all those plastic boats. Not a workboat in sight.
Alphonse darling, a dirty old fishboat is coming alongside!
Quick get out the extra bumpers. He's coming in real fast.

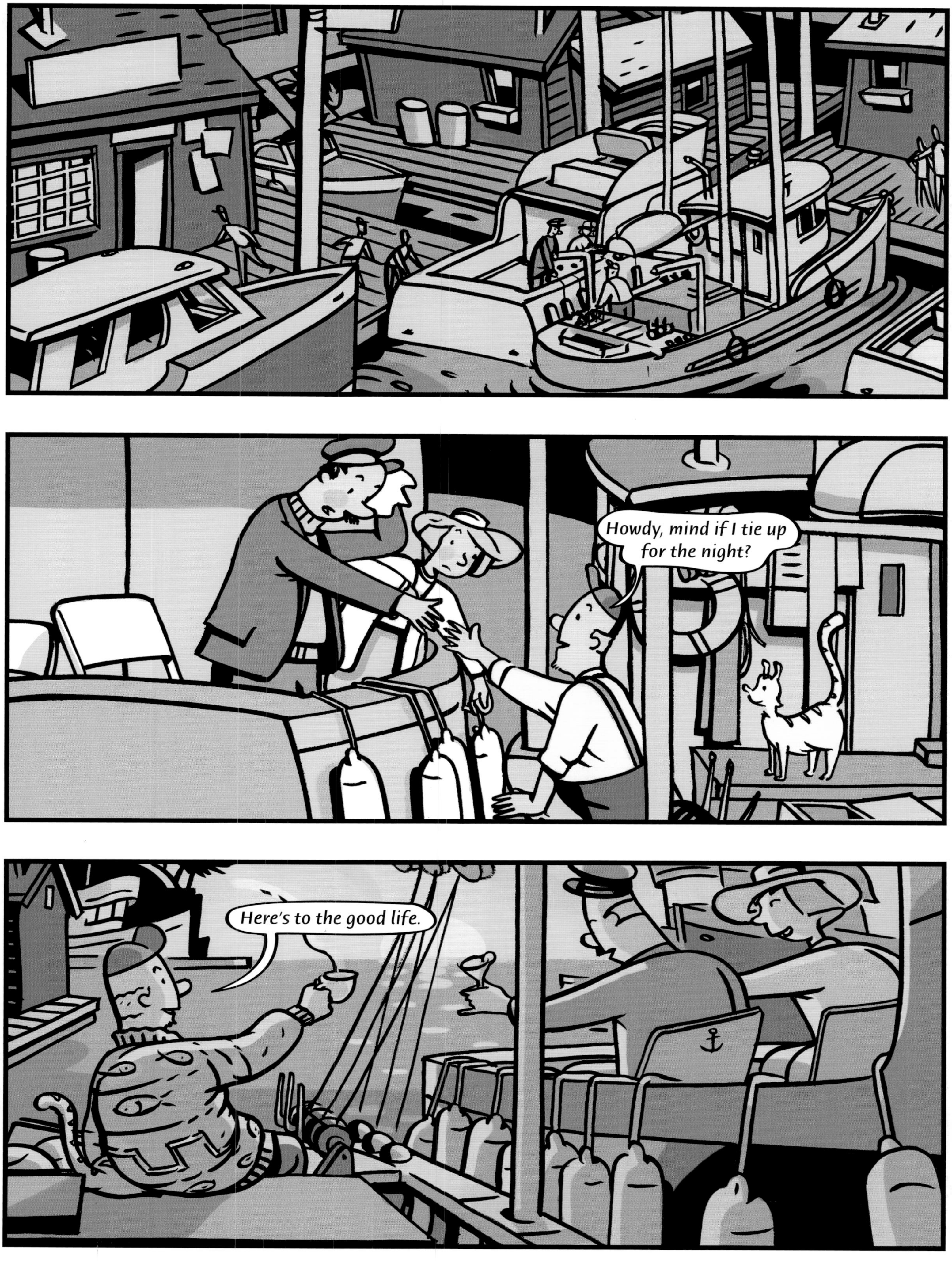
Howdy, mind if I tie up for the night?
Here's to the good life.

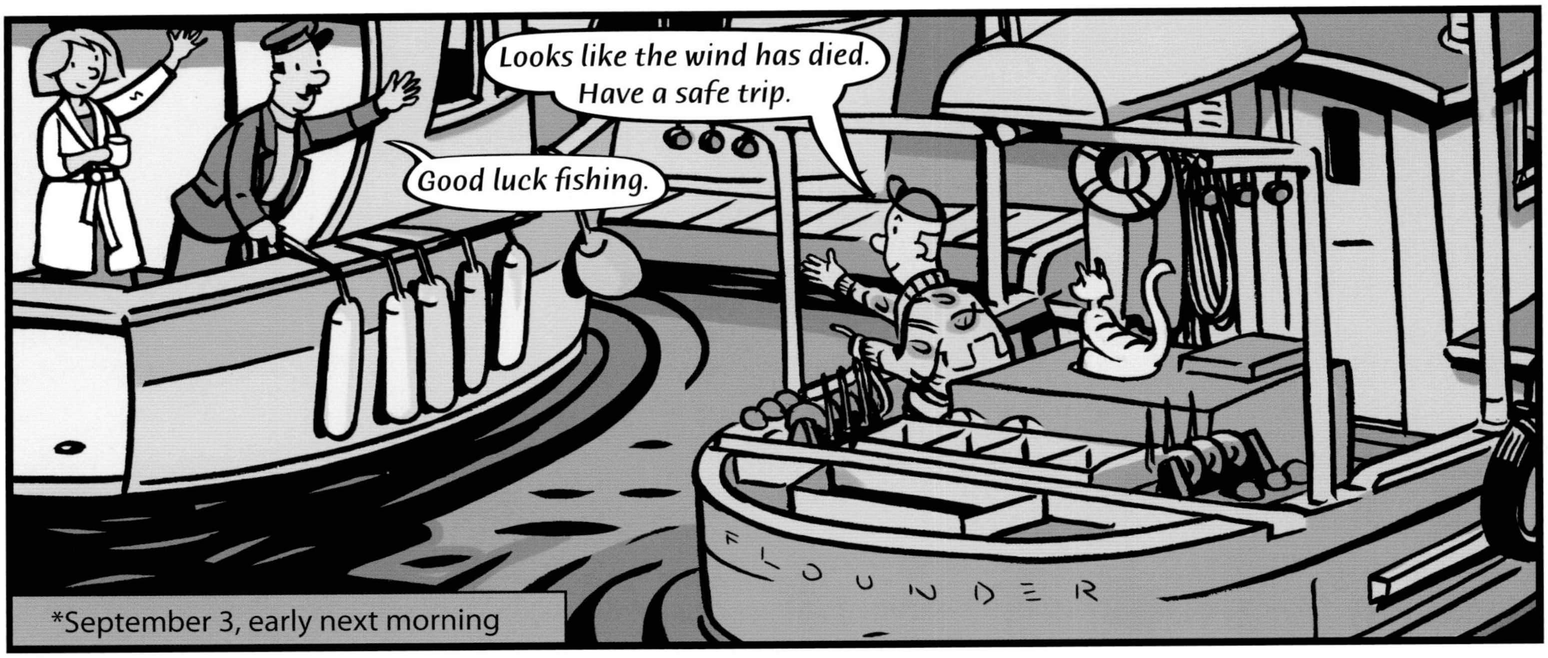
Looks like the wind has died. Have a safe trip.
Good luck fishing.
FLOUNDER
*September 3, early next morning

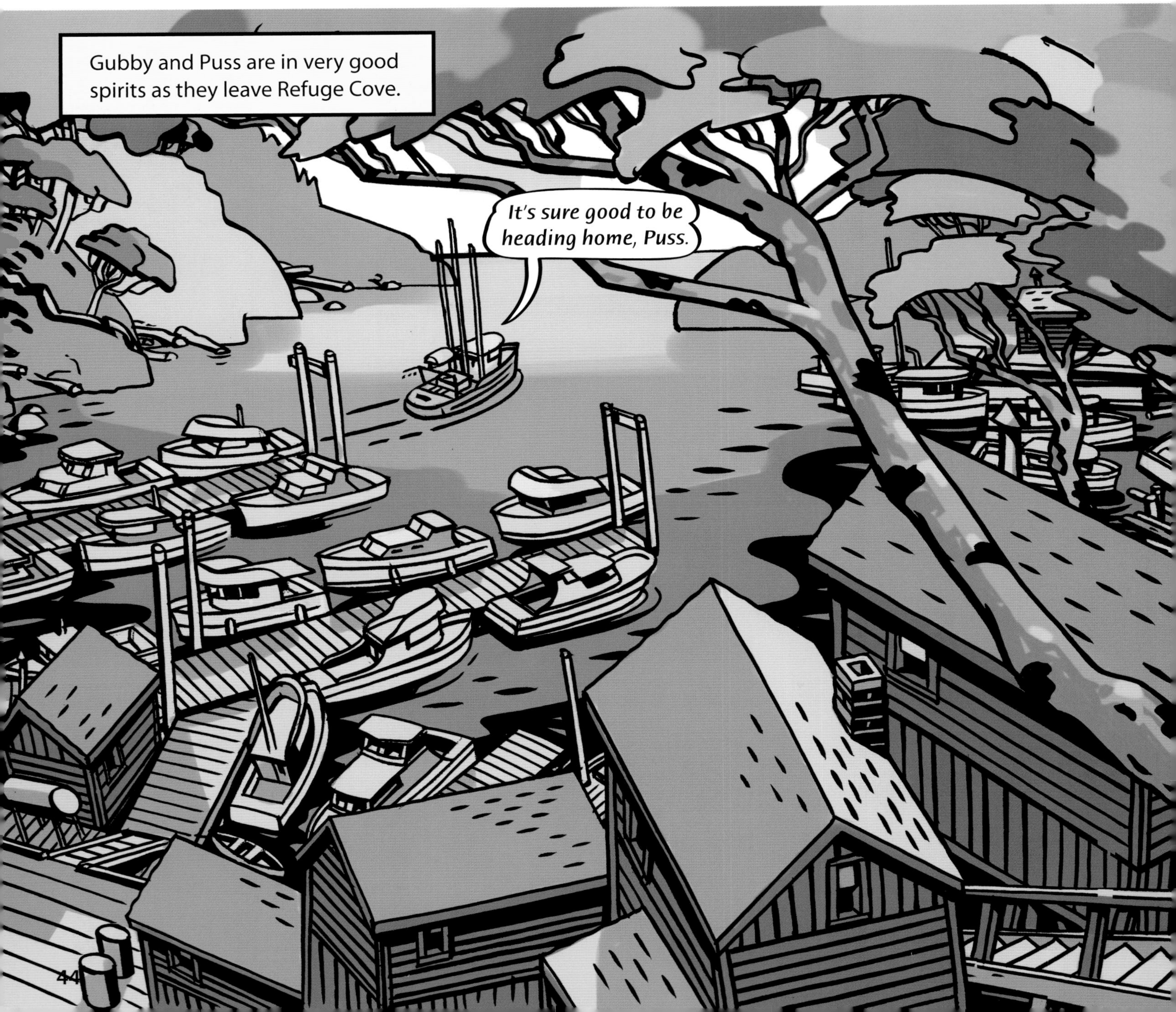
Gubby and Puss are in very good spirits as they leave Refuge Cove.
It's sure good to be heading home, Puss.

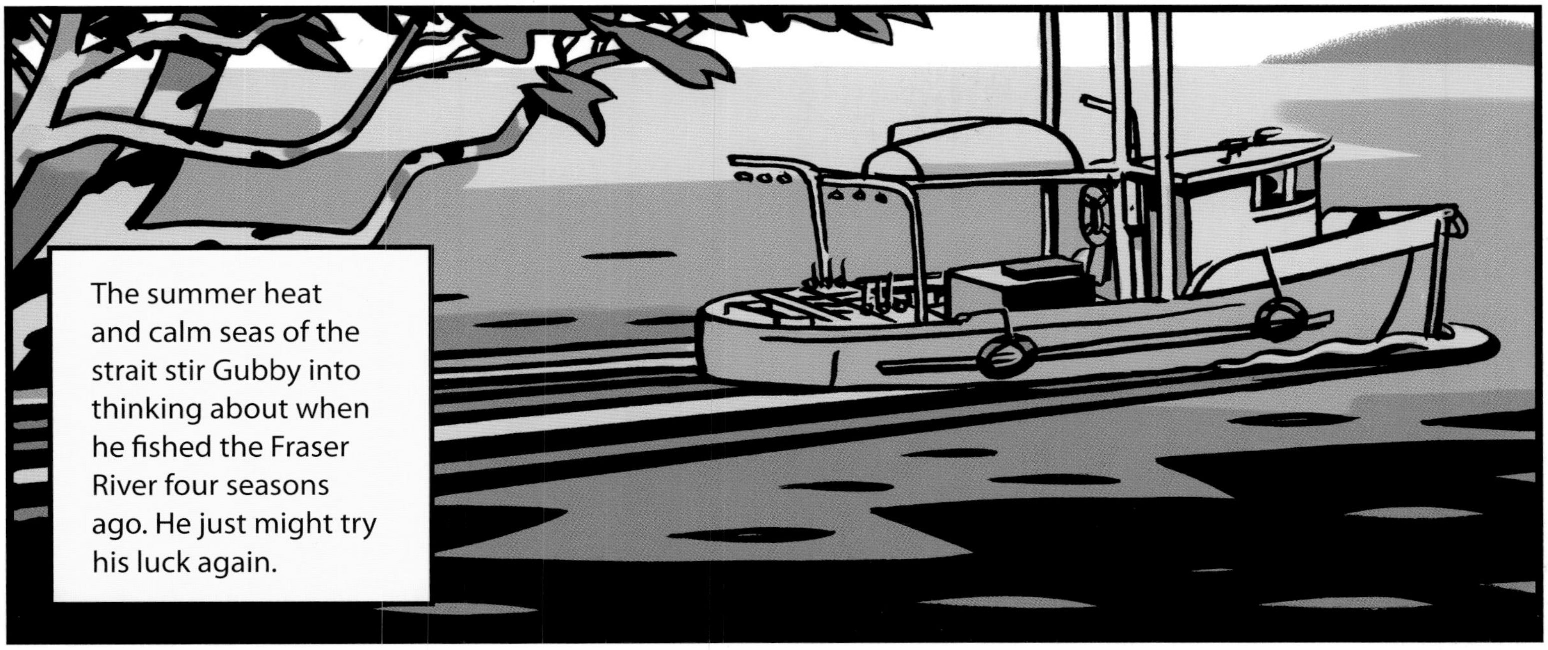
The summer heat and calm seas of the strait stir Gubby into thinking about when he fished the Fraser River four seasons ago. He just might try his luck again.

A message comes through on the radio telephone. It's Reg on the *Blue Fin*. He is wild with excitement and uses a special code so other fishermen won't know where he is fishing.

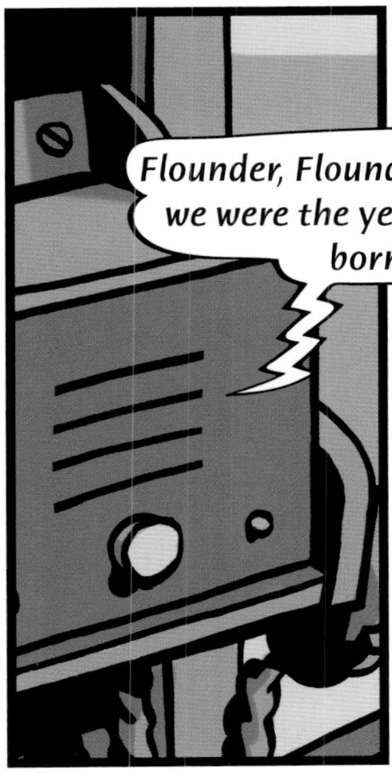
Flounder, Flounder. I'm where we were the year Puss was born.

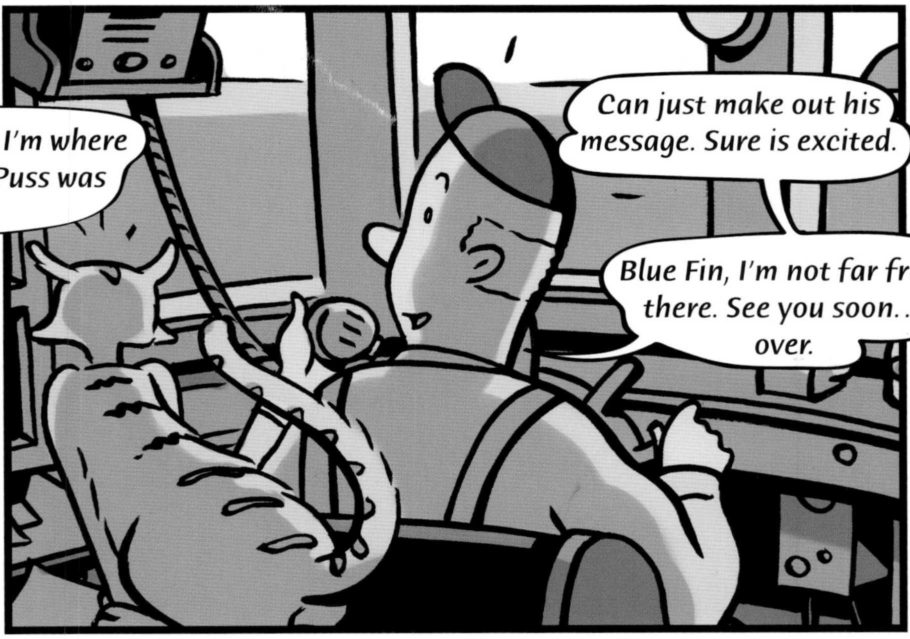
Can just make out his message. Sure is excited.
Blue Fin, I'm not far from there. See you soon... over.

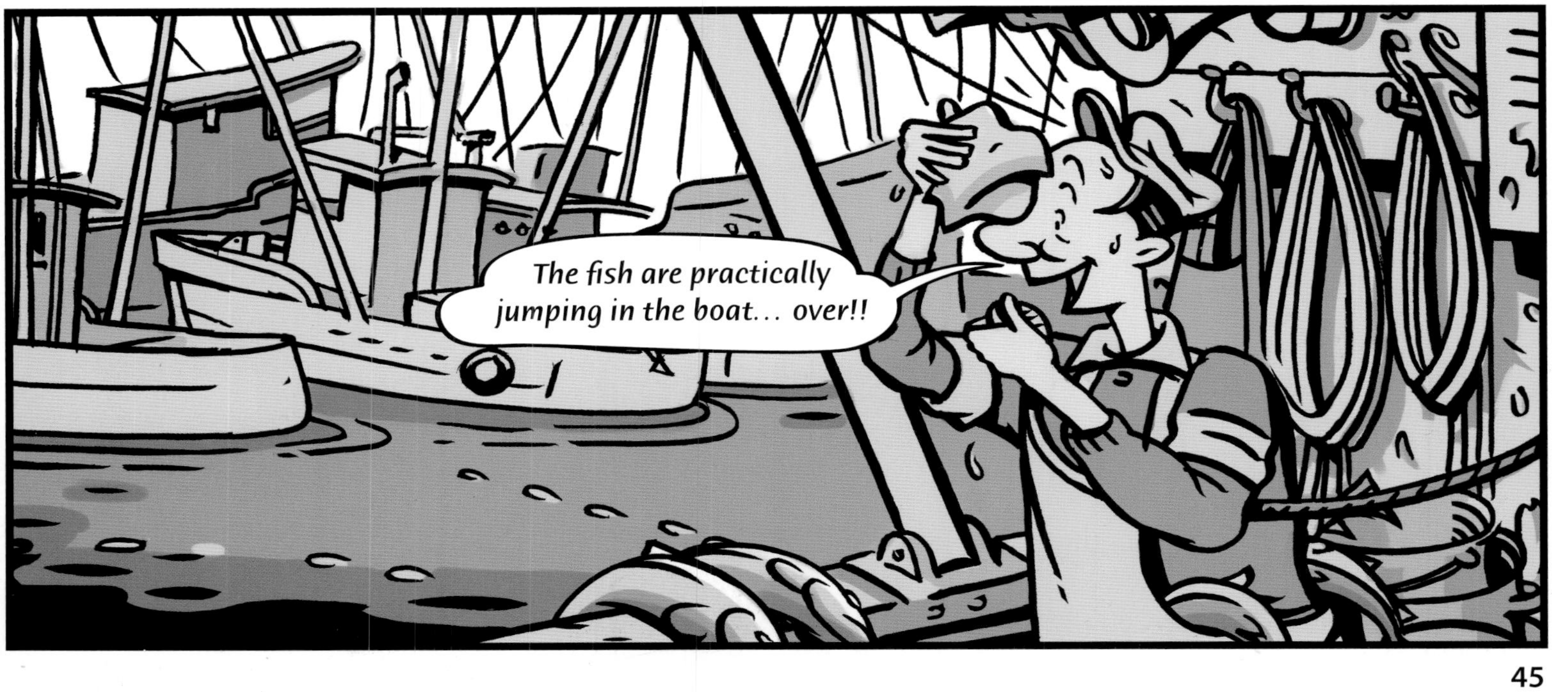
The fish are practically jumping in the boat... over!!

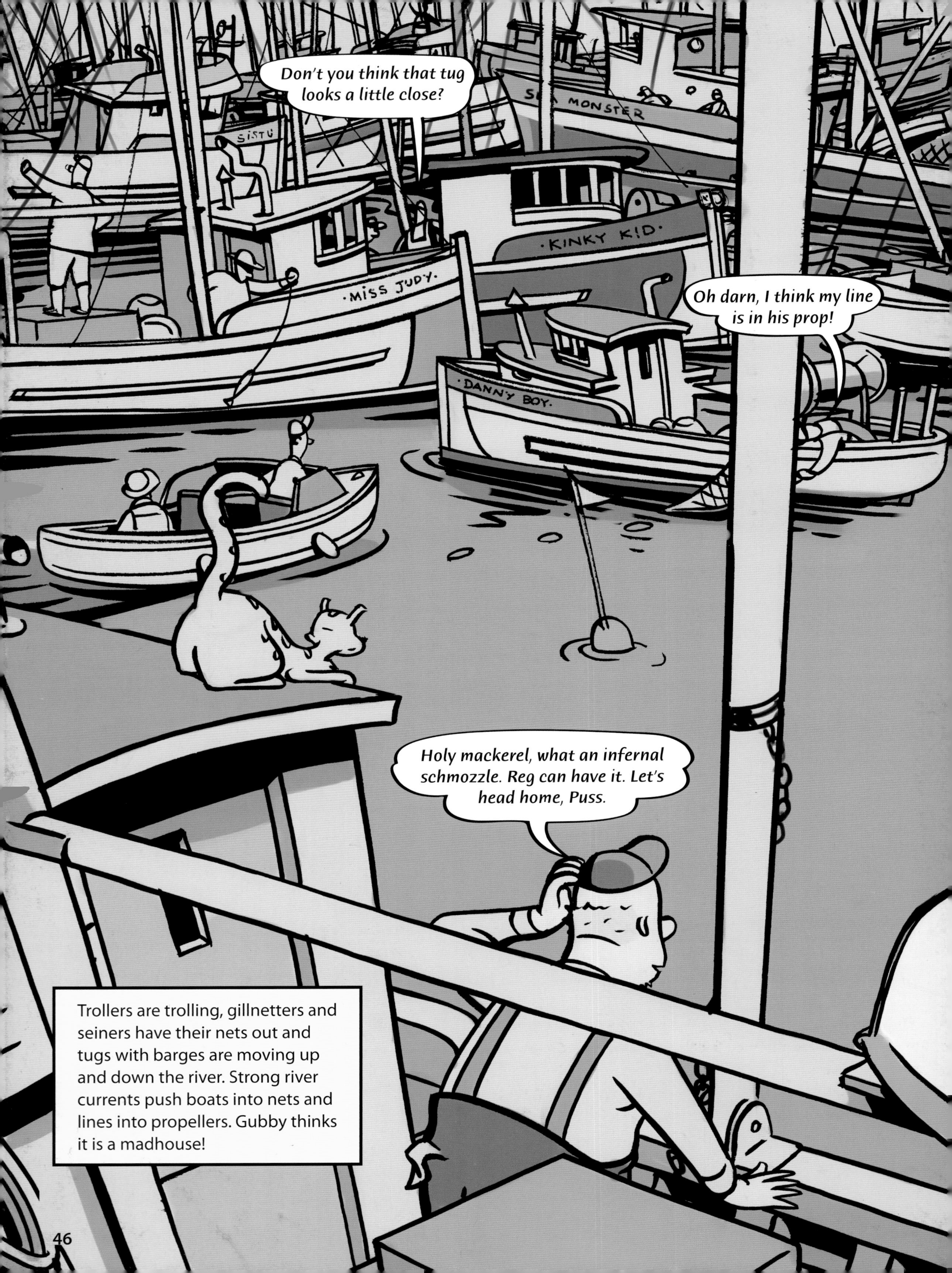
Don't you think that tug looks a little close?
·MISS JUDY·
·KINKY KID·
·DANNY BOY·
Oh darn, I think my line is in his prop!
Holy mackerel, what an infernal schmozzle. Reg can have it. Let's head home, Puss.
Trollers are trolling, gillnetters and seiners have their nets out and tugs with barges are moving up and down the river. Strong river currents push boats into nets and lines into propellers. Gubby thinks it is a madhouse!

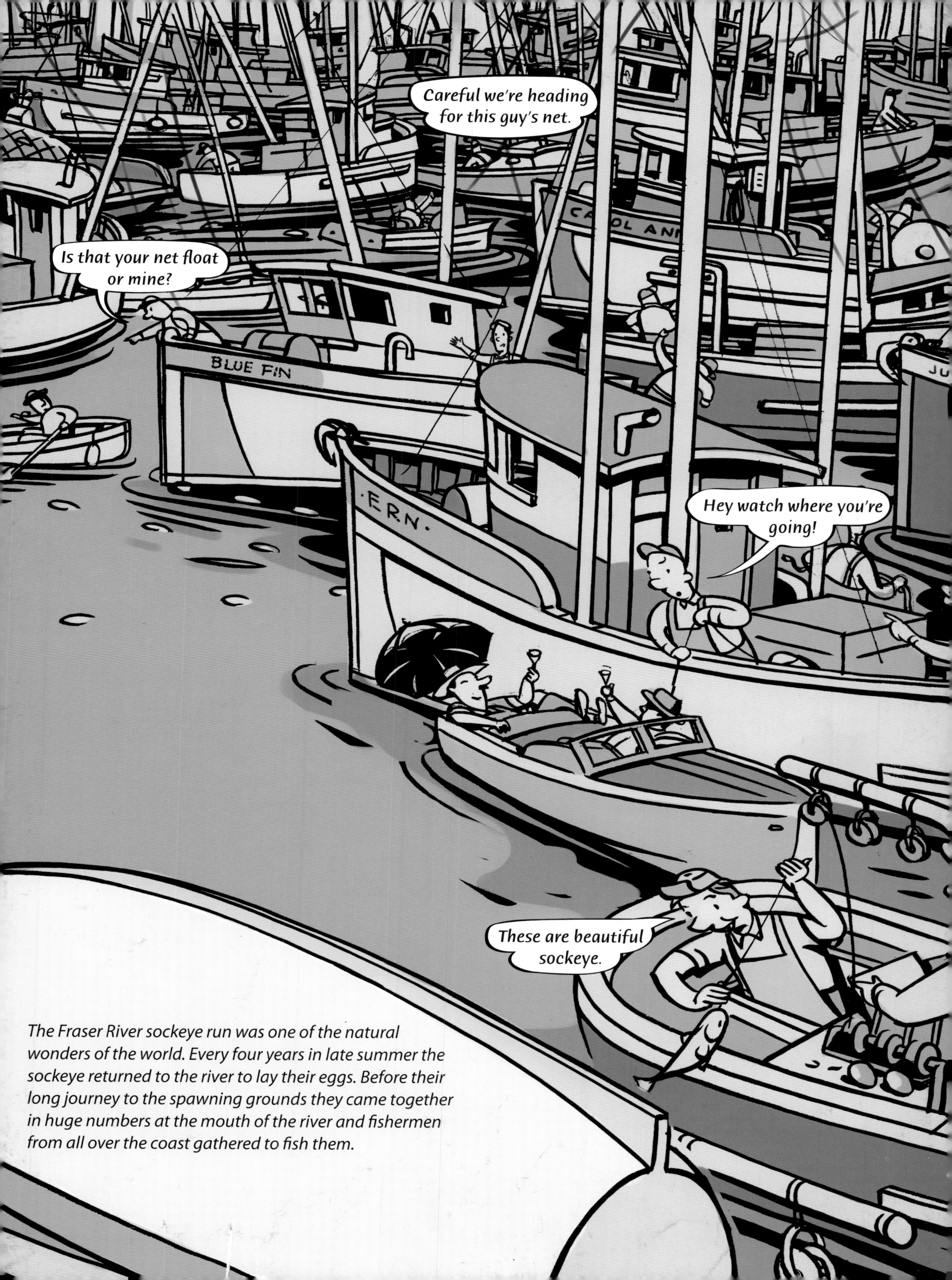
Careful we're heading for this guy's net.
Is that your net float or mine?
BLUE FIN
E.R.N.
Hey watch where you're going!
These are beautiful sockeye.
The Fraser River sockeye run was one of the natural wonders of the world. Every four years in late summer the sockeye returned to the river to lay their eggs. Before their long journey to the spawning grounds they came together in huge numbers at the mouth of the river and fishermen from all over the coast gathered to fish them.

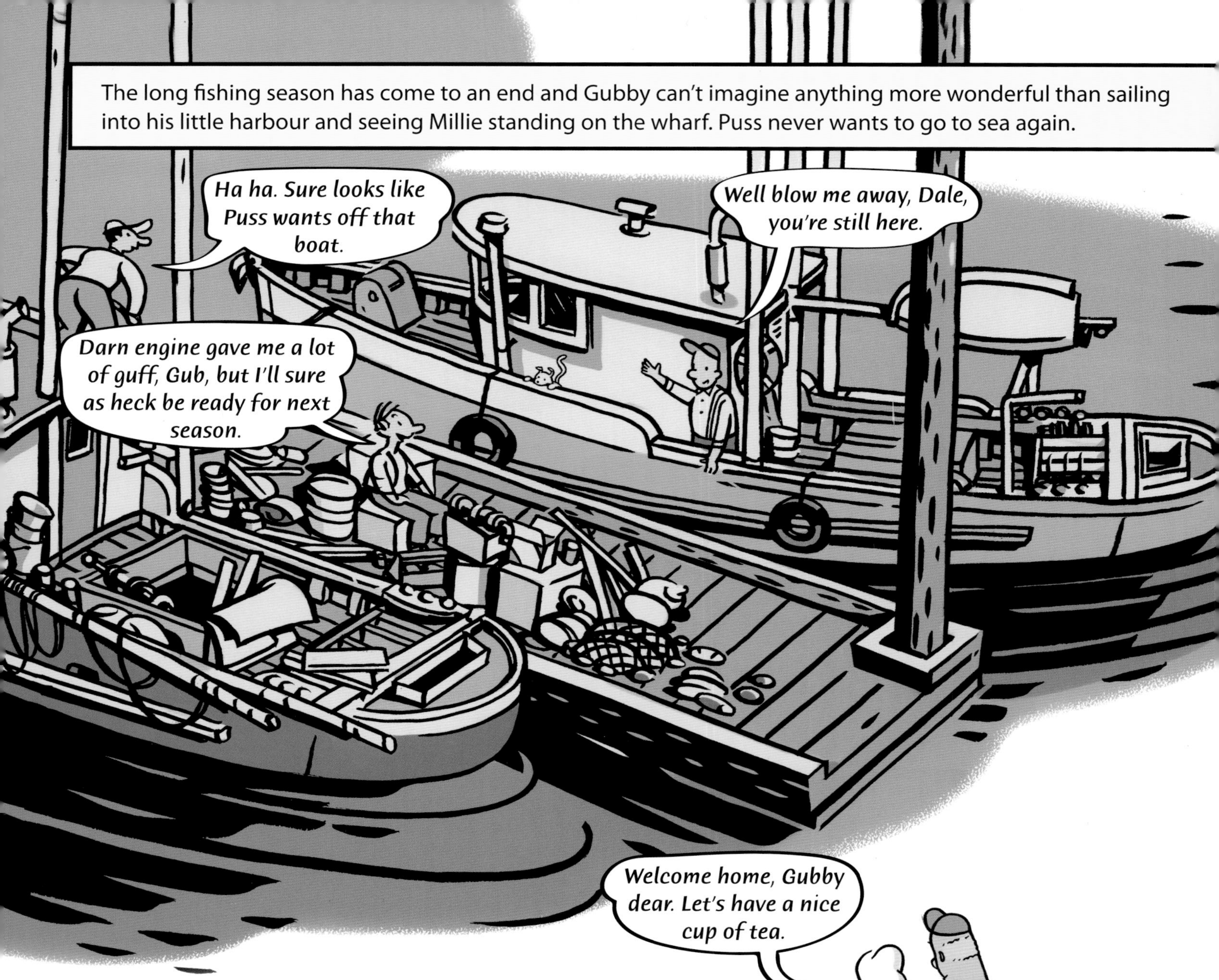

The long fishing season has come to an end and Gubby can't imagine anything more wonderful than sailing into his little harbour and seeing Millie standing on the wharf. Puss never wants to go to sea again.
Ha ha. Sure looks like Puss wants off that boat.
Well blow me away, Dale, you're still here.
Darn engine gave me a lot of guff, Gub, but I'll sure as heck be ready for next season.

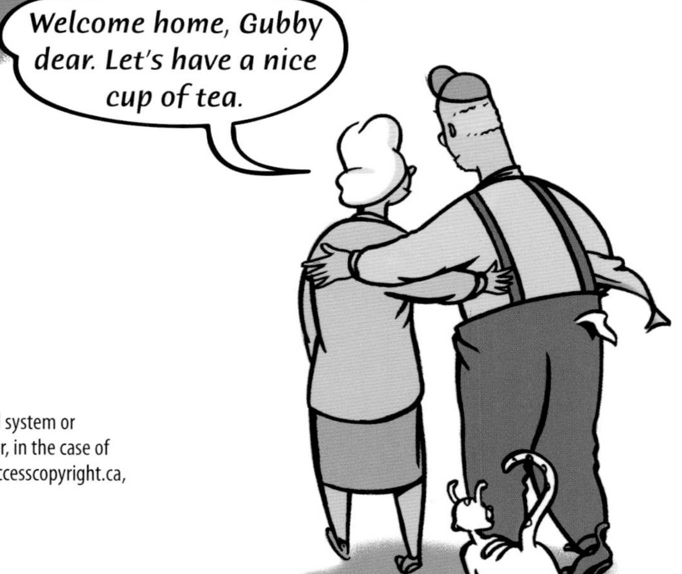

Welcome home, Gubby dear. Let's have a nice cup of tea.

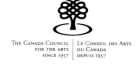

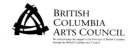

For Stacia and Bronwyn with love - Gary Kent.
For Kim, Carol, Jeff, Cameron and Chuck - KL.

1 2 3 4 5 — 14 13 12 11 10

Harbour Publishing Co. Ltd.
P.O. Box 219, Madeira Park, BC, V0N 2H0
www.harbourpublishing.com

Page layout by Kim La Fave. Art direction by Roger Handling, Terra Firma Digital Arts.
Printed on FSC-certified paper containing a combination of fibres from well-managed forests and post-consumer recycled content or other controlled forest friendly sources.
Manufactured by Prolong Press Ltd, China, August 2010, Job #02844

The Canada Council for the Arts since 1957 | Le Conseil des Arts du Canada depuis 1957

British Columbia Arts Council

Harbour Publishing acknowledges financial support from the Government of Canada through Canada Book Fund and the Canada Council for the Arts, and from the Province of British Columbia through the BC Arts Council and the Book Publishing Tax Credit.

Library and Archives Canada Cataloguing in Publication

Kent, Gary, 1941-

Fishing with Gubby / Gary Kent ; illustrated by Kim La Fave.

ISBN 978-1-55017-497-7

1. Pacific Coast (B.C.—Juvenile fiction. I. LaFave, Kim II. Title.

PS8621.E643F57 2010 jC813'.6 C2010-904245-X

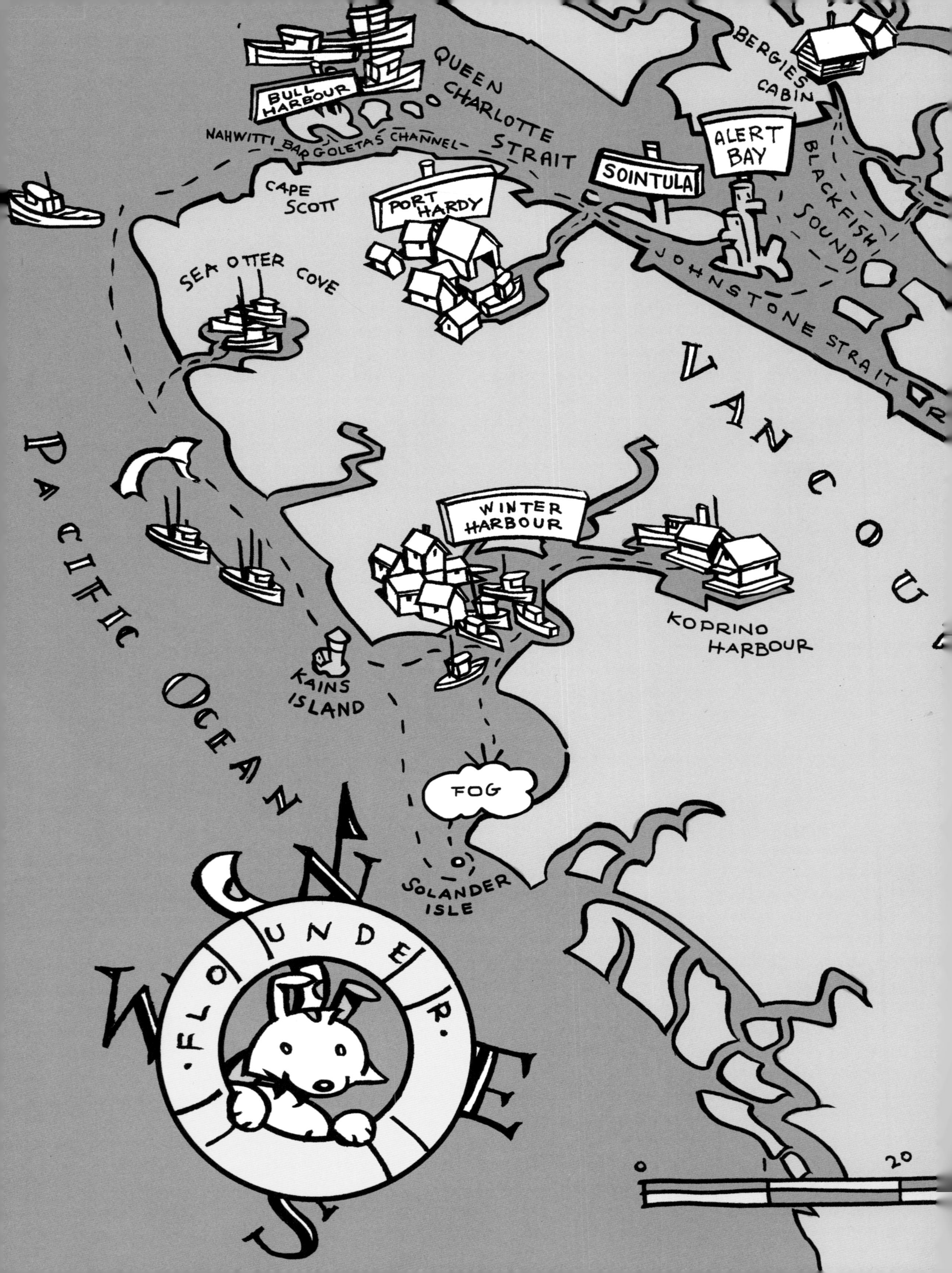
BULL HARBOUR
QUEEN CHARLOTTE STRAIT
NAHWITTI BAR
GOLETAS CHANNEL
BERGIES CABIN
ALERT BAY
SOINTULA
BLACKFISH SOUND
CAPE SCOTT
PORT HARDY
JOHNSTONE STRAIT
SEA OTTER COVE
VANCOU
PACIFIC OCEAN
WINTER HARBOUR
KOPRINO HARBOUR
KAINS ISLAND
FOG
SOLANDER ISLE
FLOUNDER
N
W
E
S
0
20